Arlen Classic Literature

Pray for the Wanderer

Kate O'Brien

PRAY FOR THE WANDERER

Foreword by Caitríona Clear

Pray for the Wanderer

is published in 2022 by
ARLEN HOUSE
42 Grange Abbey Road
Baldoyle, Dublin D13 A0F3
Ireland
Email: arlenhouse@gmail.com
www.arlenhouse.ie

978–1–85132–277–0, paperback

International distribution by
SYRACUSE UNIVERSITY PRESS
621 Skytop Road, Suite 110
Syracuse, New York
USA 13244–5290
Email: supress@syr.edu
www.syracuseuniversitypress.syr.edu

Typesetting by Arlen House

Digitisation by Marian Keyes, Susan Bennett, Alan Hayes

Cover artwork:
detail from 'Achill Horses' by Mainie Jellett
1944, oil on canvas

The publisher wishes to acknowledge
Donough O'Brien, John O'Brien and Kathy Rose O'Brien,
steadfast and passionate advocates for Kate O'Brien

FOREWORD

Caitríona Clear

'"We all take ourselves more seriously than anyone else could possibly imagine"' remarks cynical solicitor Tom Mahoney in this novel. *Pray for the Wanderer* has also been accused (by Adele Dalsimer) of taking itself too seriously. Certainly, the cast of characters is small and the action undramatic; banned author Matt Costello comes home to Ireland, stays for a while with his brother's family, has many arguments with others and with himself, and goes away again. But this novel, usually regarded by critics as Kate O'Brien's response to the banning of *Mary Lavelle* in Ireland, is much more than a discourse on culture and censorship. It explores the emotional pain of an Irish writer genuinely torn between the artistic freedom of abroad and the beguiling beauty and security of home. That home is described vividly and lovingly; Mellick, Kate O'Brien's fictional Limerick, is a 'gravely-poised city, old and quiet.' At Weir House, the Costello home place on the Shannon banks, 'Golden willows trembled by the water and a daisied bank sloped down from the lawn to the riverpath.'

Even the banal is sanctified: in the city, Woolworths' 'red face is now almost as unexceptionable as church bells or a cat on a hearthrug, and more effective perhaps than a touch of nature in making the whole world kin.' Like the setting, the characters are memorable, and teacher/social activist Nell Mahoney is, as Mary Coll has pointed out, one of Kate O'Brien's most interesting female characters.

Nell has an MA in History, and teaches in a secondary school even though she has a private income; 'rubbish' is how her sister Una describes this vocation; 'more of her nonsense' is the verdict of Tom, the aforementioned solicitor who is Nell's cousin and also her ex-fiancé. Nell loves her job, not only for itself, but for the independence it gives her. A modern 'social Catholic', she is involved in the Legion of Mary, a lay apostolic organisation founded by Frank Duff in Dublin in 1922, and regarded with suspicion by the hierarchy for many years. When the book opens, Nell is well on the way to becoming one of the tens of thousands of permanently single Irish women who taught in schools, nursed in hospitals, worked in shops and offices and formed the backbone of voluntary organisations, Irish language organisations and amateur dramatic societies until well into the 1970s. She has a 'cool and ranging mind'; her virginity is as much 'loyalty to her own intellectual workings' as it is a condition of her religious beliefs. In stark contrast to her man-pleasing sister, Una, Nell has 'a deadly way of making a man feel that he hasn't quite got her attention'. In due course Matt Costello attracts more than her attention. And even at the end of the book, when Matt feels a spasm 'almost of outrage' at the marital complacency of his brother Will and sister-in-law Una, his respect for Nell is unchanged: 'Nell had not this suavity ... he thought of her grave, strange face.' Readers can judge for themselves whether O'Brien gives Nell a happy ending, or not.

Matt first meets Nell when he arrives home from London to stay with his brother Will and sister-in-law Una and their young family, at Weir House. Kate O'Brien, Eibhear Walshe suggests, was always anxious to show British readers that not all Irish people were peasants, and in this novel, even the farming Costello family escapes this destiny. The term 'gentleman farmer' falls short of describing their way of life, where a bottle of champagne is opened to celebrate a cow's recovery from illness, dinner always takes place in the evening, and wife and children do not perform farm work of any kind. The Costellos, unlike even most big farmers' children, do not walk every day to the local national school, but are driven in a motor car to their fee-paying schools in the nearby city. Una, their mother, is a 'rose', easygoing, sensual and pretty; Matt at first prefers her 'sweet impudence' to her sister Nell's aloofness. Although Una is perceptive and sharp, she is always the perfect wife; she stops talking about politics when Will, her otherwise mild husband, reprimands her for doing so, and always drops what she is doing to attend to him. And she worries about Nell, about whom she remarks, in one of the few comical remarks in this rather serious book: '"Well the truth is that she's thirty-three, but we don't stress it."'

Another character in the book with an abiding interest in Nell, is Tom Mahoney. She describes him early in the novel with devastating accuracy: 'He has created a thing called "Tom Mahoney" which he loves building up. He's what people call a "character" ...' Tom does not go to Mass, criticises Irish Catholicism's cultural poverty, is scathing about social Catholicism and is ribald in his conversation, but he supports the Church financially and considers himself within the fold. His social class safeguards him from censure for his nonconformity, and he has at least one good friend who is a priest. Matt, by contrast, has left the Catholic Church, but appreciates its cultural significance in his life and in western civilisation in general. He is amused to recall a fellow writer in London dismissing one of Matt's Catholic-themed novels as 'a book written by an Elk for the Brother Elks': 'How many hundred million believing Catholics were there in the contemporary world? ... Bloomsbury – now that was an esoteric entity.' But the authoritarian all-pervasiveness of modern Irish Catholicism fills Matt with dismay. The novel's main target is 'de Valera's Ireland, where the artistic conscience is ignored'. Utilitarian and triumphalist, it is almost comparable to the dictatorships of Stalin and Mussolini, although de Valera is 'a more subtle dictator than most'.

There is no nostalgia in the novel for British rule; Matt, having fought for Irish freedom, desperately wants to be loyal to the state he has helped to bring into being. Irish political and cultural independence is taken for granted, in this novel, as a good thing in itself. Nell's proficiency in the Irish language is one of the qualities that sets her apart, and O'Brien proudly uses (and explains) the term *'mar a eadh'* (often anglicised as 'mor-i-ya'; the nearest translation in the modern idiom would be 'as if!'). Even the oft-quoted passage beginning: 'Oh green and trim Free State! Smug, obstinate and pertinacious little island ...' continues to remark that the 'ignorances' of the 'fledgling nation' are 'perhaps wisdom when measured against the general European plight.' But Ireland has become a state where it is necessary to surrender 'ego and integrity to nurse an implacable theory of the common good.' In the last line of the book, Una dismisses *Don Quixote* as 'absolutely deadly', meaning boring and impenetrable. It is this refusal of adventure and romance and uncertainty, more than anything else, which causes Matt to leave Ireland again.

The London literary life to which he returns is such a cliché that one wonders whether O'Brien, that most deliberate of writers, set out to portray it as such. Matt has a flat in Bloomsbury, complete with valet, and has just ended a love affair with a beautiful actress who acts in his plays and has been his 'muse'. This actress, Louise Lafleur, owes her name (it is carefully explained) to Huguenot ancestry, but the impression of an Amanda McKittrick Ros heroine remains. ('Amanda Ros' is mentioned in one of the book's arguments about culture, so O'Brien was aware of her *oeuvre*). The affair has come to an end because Louise has gone back to the vain, older, fading film star husband who helped her early in her career.

Another rather unconvincing part of the story is Tom Mahoney's 'moral lapse' of some years previously. A 'decent little shopgirl' had his child when he was a law student in Dublin; he supported the mother and child financially, and she married a tobacconist. The female shop assistant as thrilling temptress was a popular motif in songs, plays and novels all over Europe in the decades leading up to the Great War. This was part sexual fantasy and part moral panic; in real life female shop assistants were as respectable as teachers or nurses, and no more or less alluring than any other kind of worker. Women writers of the first half of the twentieth century, from Virginia Woolf to Nancy Mitford, used this occupational designation as shorthand for flashy, uneducated femininity; Kate O'Brien, alas, was no exception.

There is a chance, however, that Tom's scornful indifference to his son and condescension to his mother (he tells Matt that the 'shopgirl' used to write him 'silly, chummy letters' about 'Tommy') is supposed to be evidence of his dubious character. Children are certainly important in this story. The young Costellos have names and personalities (even 'plain' and 'boring' Maire is individuated, albeit cruelly), they accompany the adults on outings and picnics, and are sought out and 'spoiled' (even Maire) by their uncle and aunt. Matt and Nell have their first honest conversation about their mutual attraction when they have brought ten-year-old Liam out on a drive (he is conveniently out of earshot). Liam is what used to be called an 'old-fashioned child' – generous, sensitive, serious, with an overdeveloped sense of responsibility. But for all his striving after goodness, he goes to school in dread every day, and gets six strokes of a cane on his hands at school for 'insolence' (trying to explain why he had the wrong colour copybook). Una, cutting up Liam's food for him because his hands are temporarily disabled, comforts him: '"You know we all think in this house ... that it's a bad idea, people caning and hurting each other ... But the Jesuits evidently think we're wrong ..."'

The novel's title is taken from the very popular Marian hymn 'Hail Queen of Heaven', which Matt hears when he goes to collect Nell and the children from Benediction one glorious summer evening. There, he makes a decision to change his life forever, but despite his love for the people and places of Ireland, he has to go back 'alone into the places of doom and panic and despair'. Unanchored by the familiar and the loved, the wanderer needs prayers so as to maintain courage and integrity. But every Catholic reading the book's title would follow the hymn onto the next line, which is the simple appeal, 'Pray for me'. Exiled, banned writers might be culturally triumphant in the long run, but they are excluded and lonely. In *Pray for the Wanderer* the sadness of this exclusion is a far more predominant note than anger.

ADDITIONAL READING

Mary J. Coll, 'Kate O'Brien: a study of the social environment in her novels', MA Thesis, University College Galway 1985.

Adele M. Dalsimer, *Kate O'Brien: A Critical Study* (Dublin, Gill & Macmillan, 1990).

Eibhear Walshe, *Kate O'Brien: A Writing Life* (Dublin, Irish Academic Press, 2006).

Pray for the Wanderer

The First Chapter

A heron peered out of the poplar. There always had been a heron in that tree. Linda used to call it 'Sister Anne.' The river was full, and northward, before it vanished, went over the weir in a high light. Golden willows trembled by the water and a daisied bank sloped down from the lawn to the river path. To stand at this window again was not more real than to remember standing there.

'How long do herons live, Liam?'

'I don't know, Uncle Matt. But there's a bird book here. Shall I look it up?'

'Sixteen years, do you think?'

The little boy laughed as he knelt before the bookshelves.

'Surely not as long as that,' he said. 'That's six years older than me.'

'Do you find great changes here, Matt?'

Matt Costello smiled reflectively at his brother, and then at the room; the wood fire, the Victorian sofa, pink flowers on the wallpaper, the old brass cake stand. He thought what a surefire laugh that would be in a certain kind of play. 'Ah, the dear old cake stand!' At teatime his sister-in-law's smooth white hand on its handle had suddenly become before his eyes his mother's hand. He had seen the big knuckles and veins, the yellowing, bony wrist.

'Yes. No,' he said to Will. 'Actually, no. Because Liam and Maire and Sean and the rest of them are us after all – you and me and Linda and Joe and Dolly. And Una is mother, and you're father. So it's all the same – repeating itself very rightly. No, I think that I'm the only novelty I find, the only oddity.'

'Will's face moved into a greater, shyer kindliness.

'You mustn't say that, dear chap. You're at home here. Nothing odd in that.'

'I've found the heron, Uncle Matt, but there's nothing about the age it lives to.'

'Ah! That's the worst of reference books. They never tell you the only thing you want to know.'

'Do you really think so?' Liam looked anxious. 'Because you know I find them very useful.'

Just like Will to say that, and in that nervous way of affection. 'You're at home here.' He was a family man. Backward in respect to his parents, laterally in anxiety for his brothers and sisters, forward in tender hope to his children, all that he was flowed out on those blood channels. They were his circuit, limited but warm. He did not believe that a human life could be lived satisfactorily on any other track, and if a man of thirty-seven had not found that only good, had not established himself in piety among his natural household gods, if Will cared for that man with an elder brother's tenderness, he was sensitive to cover his bad luck from him. Matt was not repeating the good pattern, had no home. Will, sorry for that, must cover any hint of pain by pretending therefore that he had and that it was here, that he was in fact in his old place in the old pattern of their particular childhood now grown so dim, now indeed replaced by bright new threads. Will did not see that life might fruitfully be a lonely track or a jealously personal adventure. He did not see how a man could, or could be glad to, circumvent the blood emotions. Save, of course, under the mysterious imperative of the religious life. Nor did he see, even to gasp at it, even to combat it, that Europe, the Western world, was like his brother Matt, afraid, and growing tired of what was for him the sweetest natural law. He did not see where the frightened world had got to. He was not frightened. He was a citizen of the Irish Free State, and a family man. And Matt, taking his kindly smile now, thought that as Sodom and Gomorrah might have been saved by five good men, so perhaps, perhaps the warm personal principle now about to die, perhaps the individualistic thing, the piled-up memory, the piety, the long-held, bitterly-wronged sweetness of personal liberty now going over everywhere, the one good light going out – might yet be saved by a few men of blind good sense, who knew not what they did. A few more Wills innocently cultivating their gardens, and the old beaten principle might be accidentally, paradoxically saved for Liam and Maire and Sean.

'Sherry? You're a connoisseur, I suppose, but this is quite good.'

Matt tasted it.

'It's very good.'

'Could I have a little, father – in honour of Uncle Matt coming home?'

'By no means, Liam. In honour of nothing.'

Una, Will Costello's wife, came into the room.

'Yes, thank you, Will, I'll have a little sherry. Oh, Liam darling, *will* you put away your stamps! You know they shouldn't be in the drawing room at all.'

'But, Mother, there's no *room* in the playroom, I tell you! Sean's silly old bricks and –'

'Tidy them up before dinner, like a good boy. I am afraid this is a haphazard house for a finicky author to come to, Matt!'

'Who said Matt was finicky?' asked Will.

'Authors are finicky, I believe. Aren't they, Matt?'

'So you all say. Where are you going to sit, Una?'

She sat at the end of the sofa and smiled up prettily at Matt, who brought her her sherry. He remembered his first meeting with her in Paris when she was on her honeymoon with Will twelve years ago. A wild and blowy rose. She was still an innocently seductive woman, plump and rather charmingly untidy, with mousy hair and a fragrance of contentment.

'Nell is late, and you must be starving. As they reported you were asleep at lunchtime we didn't send you up a tray.'

'But you saw how terrifically I ate at tea.'

'He *was* asleep during lunch, Mother. I crept in and took a really steady stare at him,' said Liam.

'Oh God, how terrible for me.'

'You've shaved since then, haven't you?'

'Yes.'

'Anyone could tell.'

'Liam, that will do, darling. Did you really sleep, Matt? Did the river disturb you? We're so used to it. It really is an appalling journey from Euston by night.'

'Yes. I should have come by day. But the idea of starting a long journey in the small hours –'

Will laughed.

'Small hours! 8.45am. It's well you didn't decide to be a farmer, my boy.'

'Very well.'

'Aunt Nell said she couldn't be here until a quarter-past seven, because of Grand-aunt Hannah's bridge party – do you remember, Mother?'

'Yes. But it's that time now. Nell will be tired – and cranky – after that awful party.'

'Shall I tell her you said she'd be cranky?'

'Tell her what you like, young man.'

'You remember Nell, don't you, Matt? Una's sister?' Matt looked politely uncertain. When Una married Will, Matt had been vague about the Mahoney girls, with whom it seemed he had played musical chairs at Christmas parties.

'But, of course, you're thirty-seven, so Nell mightn't have been around in your time. How old *is* she, Una?'

'Well, the truth is that she's thirty-three, but we don't stress it.'

'It's exactly seven-fifteen,' said Will.

'And that's the horn of her car,' shouted Liam, and darted from the room.

Exactly seven-fifteen. Matt closed his eyes. She was leaving for the theatre now. At the very door of the flat she was pulling on her coat. Carelessly, carelessly. She was going downstairs to find a taxi. Frowning a very little. Beginning to be her part. Louise, Louise.

There was commotion in the hall where through the open drawing room door Nell Mahoney could be seen trying to get out of her coat while four children pulled at her. The little girl of the four was clutching a brown paper bag.

'Whipped cream walnuts – is that all right?'

'Oh, thank you, Auntie.'

'Whom are they for, Aunt Nell?' said Sean.

'All of you. Work it out peaceably.'

Una was on the threshold now, hiding the group.

'Sweets again? Really, Nell, you're training them to be pigs! Come and meet your distinguished brother-in-law.'

The two women came into the room. 'This is the famous Matt Costello. My sister Nell.'

The present too shook hands.

'Good evening, Nell,' said Will.

'Good evening, Will.'

'Nell is a pretty good highbrow, Matt,' Will went on. 'One of the best that Mellick can do any way. That's why we asked her out here to dine your very first night. You see, Una and I are a little bit frightened!'

'Well, we thought you'd require conversation anyhow – and we're weak in that. Sherry, Nell?'

'No, thank you.' She looked at Matt. 'An appalling way to introduce two people,' she said with a detachment, even a refusal of humour, which took his attention. Her eyes were grey.

'Yes, it's dreadful,' he agreed, and was conscious of an intention to make her smile as he spoke, 'but it braces one up, don't you think, like harsh brandy.'

She did smile.

'I don't know much about brandy,' she said. 'Is it an irritant?'

Neat, Matt conceded. She had not liked the manner of her presentation to him, and was not going to condone it.

'Una Bán is too young for whipped cream walnuts, isn't she, Mother?' Maire still clutched the bag.

'Anyway, she's asleep,' said Liam.

'My pets,' said Una, 'do please promise to eat only *one* each tonight – and eat them now, before you wash your teeth.'

'Una Bán's asleep,' said Peadar gently, embracing his father's knee.

Will bent and picked up the four-year-old.

'So is Peadar, I think,' he said.

'Mother said you might be cranky after the bridge party,

Aunt Nell. Are you?'

Nell laughed.

'I am.'

'Aunt Hannah lost her boots, as usual, I suppose?' said Will.

'Yes. A gloomy business.'

The children smiled delightedly.

'Was she very cross, Aunt Nell? Before all the other people?'

'You're a lot of dreadful little gossips,' said Nell.

A large red woman in a white apron appeared in the doorway.

'Bedtime,' said Una, 'here's Bridie. Come on, Bridie, tumble them off. No, Liam, you can't sit up during dinner tonight –'

'You said while Uncle Matt was here –'

'I said *sometimes* while Uncle Matt was here; but you're going to early Mass tomorrow, and you were up late last night –'

A gong pealing in the hall made chaos of good nights and arguments. Everyone was kissed by the four children, and Una promised to visit them in bed. Meanwhile the group crossed the hall and the grownups entered the dining room.

'Good night again, old chap.'

'Good night, Aunt Nell.'

'Good night, Liam.'

'Good night, Uncle Matt, good night.'

The dining room seemed to have changed less in sixteen years than had the drawing room. Naturally both rooms had been renewed in paint and paper many times and had suffered alterations of detail – but this the fewer, Matt imagined. The colours struck him nostalgically, and he remembered most of the furniture. The silver trophies, too, behind the glass doors of the Chippendale cupboards, were mainly, though Will had added to their number, old familiars.

John Costello, their father, breeder of blood stock, had owned some famous brood mares and a world-renowned stallion. Oil paintings of some of these – extraordinarily bad pictures in pleasant gilt frames – still hung on the dining room wall. Matt smiled at them and was tempted to ask Will – who had abandoned thoroughbred horses for thoroughbred cattle – whether he should not have some portraits done of his Dairy Shorthorns, but he dropped the joke lest it should seem to sneer.

'Anyhow, Will, here's one change I notice with definite pleasure – though indeed it surprises, almost shocks me!'

'What's that?'

'That you've actually abandoned the pious ancestral habit of farmhouse tea. Dinner at night, thank God!' Matt laughed gratefully towards Una. 'Your doing?'

'My doing.'

'When I married Matt it was made clear to me that none of the grand Mahoneys could be expected to sit down to tea and cold ham at the end of the day.'

'Barbarous custom!'

'It was a good meal, I always thought, when we were kids.'

'Grand, when we were kids. But middle-aged and dyspeptic – oh, Una, I'm very glad you have the whip hand.'

'It's the only thing I've been bullied about, I believe.' Will smiled at his wife.

'Is he right, Una?'

'Will is always right.' Her eyes teased both men lazily. Matt pondered her innocent unfoldedness of nature, the ease with which her untricked and native seduction spread its perfume. She was fading, but would live and die most recognisably a rose. And this other, this sister – what flower is she, he wondered, and chuckled a little inwardly over his album game. Impossible to place her yet in a Tennysonian garden. She withheld, was in the sheath, and perhaps would only condescend to flower for a very violent and especial sun. Amused by his extravagantly sentimental idea, he looked at her cautiously.

She was probably about the same height as her sister but was so slim and sat with so straight a grace that she appeared more than common tall. Her mouse-fair hair, heavy and soft, was brushed away from her forehead and curled up softly at the tips. Her face was difficult to assess, and quite unlike her sister's. She was white-skinned, and delicate-seeming of texture; in spite of the 'visor down' expression of her eyes, her features yielded a very light, very accurate flexibility of reaction to transient matters. Clearly nothing escaped her – she had the eyelids of a commentator – but, probably acknowledging that herself also must, by human lot, be up for comment, she still preferred to make her bid for escape, essential escape. She would never, like her sister, appear to be at the heart of any warm, open, intimate moment – but she did not seem shy. Certainly she was neither gauche nor nervous, but had a tranquillity which differed from Una's in that it was non-voluptuous and probably rose from a habit of reflection. She might indeed be something of a wit, Matt conceded, with that queer, thin face, which suggested itself as a possible mask for a number of comically contrasted people – Madame du Deffand, for instance, he thought mischievously – or Saint Catherine of Siena. Or some might have said Sappho. Obviously not commonplace, since across a quiet dining table and by saying almost nothing she suggested such a variety of comparisons. He thought that it would be interesting to see her drunk, and then almost started in amused shock. Could he so soon forget that he was at home in Mellick, where no lady is ever drunk, even in 1937? How civilised that is, he conceded; most excellently sophisticated. Meantime, among his cosmopolitan friends would this woman who sat opposite be accounted beautiful or not? There would be clever remarks. Shield herself as she might, she was a target for them. Some might rave and find her Etruscan; some, very silly, would say that she was sheer Toulouse Lautrec; a few might think that she was just odd and out of drawing.

'Such trout I haven't eaten in a lifetime, Una!'

'Liam caught them. Indeed, if I'd remembered that I'd have let him sit up to watch us eat them. Be sure to tell him tomorrow that they were absolutely delicious.'

'The dapping is good this year,' said Will.

'You'll come on the lake tomorrow, won't you? You're just in time for the last of the mayfly.'

'I'd love to go on the lake, but I refuse to fish – and thank you kindly.'

'Good God! What *will* you do? Write poetry?'

'I don't think so.'

'Of course he won't fish. I tell you what, Will, we'll all drive up there and make tea in Quinlan's field –'

'But, Una, the kids will want to get into the boat and really –'

'I won't let them get in – I promise.'

'Liam may. He's a fisherman.'

'That reminds me,' Nell looked directly at Matt. 'Tom sent earnest messages. He's determined to see you tomorrow. Tom Mahoney, our cousin.'

'Tom Mahoney!' Matt paused to remember, and smiled in broad pleasure. 'Good Heavens! Is he in Mellick at present? Is he your cousin?'

Everyone seemed faintly surprised.

'Of course he's in Mellick,' said Will. 'Where else would

he be? He's a Mellick man, damn it.'

'Didn't you know he's our cousin?' Una was amused and explanatory. 'You're really very vague, Matt. What have you been dreaming about all these years? Our Aunt Hannah, of whom you've heard us talking tonight, is Tom's mother – and Nell and I were brought up in her house in King's Crescent. She still lives there – you must remember going to our parties in your velvet suit! I remember you. You see, our father and mother died when Nell and I were tiny. We always lived with Aunt Hannah.'

'Yes. Yes, of course. And Tom – where does he live?'

'With Aunt Hannah too, of course. He's her only child. A lazy, spoilt individual.' Una chuckled. 'Oh, do have some more peas!'

'What's he doing? He read law, didn't he?' He and Tom Mahoney had been at the university together.

'Yes, he's a solicitor, and very well off. God knows how, because I never knew anyone who seems to take life so easy.'

'Oh, he has an old family practice,' said Will. 'There's hardly a farmer in the county takes his litigation anywhere else but to Mahoney's office.'

Matt smiled musingly. He would be glad to see that man.

'What's he like?' he said directly to Nell. He thought that some part of her shrank a little from the question but she answered amusedly.

'Picturesque – and eloquent. And rather larger than life size.'

'Picturesque? Tom?' Una seemed greatly tickled.

'He has created a thing called "Tom Mahoney" which he loves building up,' Nell went on. 'He's what people call a "character" I suppose.'

Matt noticed that Una looked with attention at her sister and then cocked an eyebrow at her husband, who smiled back vaguely.

'He's rather young to be a "character" surely,' she said. 'He's only your age, Matt.'

'Oh, "characters" are born,' said Nell. 'Don't you think?' she challenged Matt.

'I suppose so. But he was more than that. He was an intellectual.'

'He'd like to hear you say it – in that tone. Is an "intellectual" the ultimate good thing to be then?'

A Daniel come to judgment. Matt felt a little bored.

'A true intellectual – yes, I think so.'

'God help me in that case!' said Will amusedly.

'God help us all,' said Matt. 'But when *shall* I see Tom?' he asked Nell.

'He leaves that to you, and hopes that you'll telephone. But he'd like tomorrow, in the later part of the day.'

'Tom says that the sun always rises at five pm,' said Will.

'I'll tell you what,' said Una. 'You drive him up to the lake to us tomorrow afternoon, Nell. We'll be there about four – an hour before sunrise – and tell him from me that a cup of tea will make a nice change.'

Nell demurred. 'He doesn't like family life.'

'Well, he needn't have it. He can sit on a rock with Matt and quote Plato at the top of his voice. Women and children won't compete.'

'That sounds lively. Will you tell him that I'll be at the lake at four o'clock?'

'Very well. If he doesn't like the arrangement he can telephone you before lunch.'

'Thank you. Yes, Una, I love asparagus.'

'Our own. We're proud of it this year.'

A clock on the mantelpiece chimed eight strokes. Half an hour, please. Half an hour, Miss Lafleur. Her head was swathed in a towel, and her face shone with greasepaint. Her features were strained and seemed further apart than was natural. Once he had told her that at this point in the makeup process she became a very silly wax model of herself.

'This fellow's play is still running to full houses,' Will was saying to Nell.

'Oh, not quite full houses. But it's doing very well – touch wood.'

'How long has it been on now?' Nell asked. 'I've forgotten when the first night was.'

'We had our hundredth night on 21st April – that's five weeks ago.'

'Will – you and I simply must go over and see I. Do you think it will run till September, which is the only time of the year when I can move this farmer of mine?'

'I daren't say – but really you know, it might.'

'We didn't go to your first night this time, old chap,' said Will, 'because we were beginning to think that perhaps we were hoodoos for you. You've had such bad luck before after good first nights –'

'I know. But I missed you all the same. Hometown backing is helpful somehow on those ghastly occasions.'

'I'm dying to see it,' said Una.

He laughed.

'You won't like it, Una.'

'I suppose not. I – I'm afraid I don't like the things you write about as a rule. But I must see it. Why did you give it that name – *The Heart of Stone?*'

'Don't you like it?'

'No – horrid.'

'Will it ever be printed?' Nell asked.

'Yes. It's coming out in a few weeks. But it will be censored in this country.'

''Tch, 'tch. I wish you weren't always censored,' said Una. 'What's the fun of having a famous relative if he's got to be so embarrassing?'

'We'll make him settle down over here, Una, and learn sense.' Will's manner was very kind and a little embarrassed. He did not read his brother's novels and plays, though proud of his success, but he hated having to face, however lightly, the knowledge that a member of his family was frequently guilty of impropriety in print.

'What kind of play is it?' Nell asked. 'Tragedy?'

'It is intended as high comedy. It's an analysis of emotional aridity.'

'Indeed?' said Will.

'Emotional aridity?' Nell's eyes were very grey and unconcerned. 'Don't the words contradict each other?'

'Perhaps. Really, it's just a comedy about despair.'

Una chuckled. 'You're clever if you can make a comedy about that.'

'I'm clever all right.'

'And it's well acted? You're pleased with your cast?'

'Tremendously pleased. They're grand.'

'The leading lady seems to be very good,' said Nell.

'Oh yes – her photographs are lovely. Do tell us about her!' Una was eager. 'Louise Lafleur! Such a fantastic name. Almost absurd, don't you think? Wherever did she get it?'

'At the font. It's her own name, funnily enough.'

'No?'

'Yes. She's of Huguenot descent.'

'I thought all the Huguenots were massacred.'

'Not the Lafleurs, Una.'

'A society woman, I suppose,' said Will, looking knowing. 'All actresses are nowadays, aren't they?'

'Well, they all do come from some section of society.

Miss Lafleur's father was a greengrocer in a small way in Dover, and after school hours she used to help deliver the carrots and onions round the district.'

'And now she's a great star! Marvellous! How old is she?'

'Thirty-two. It's what people call a romantic story. She had some sort of childish talent for speaking verse, I think; she also had fantastic dreams and great strength of will. And when she was sixteen she got herself attached, as some kind of odd man out, to a fourth-rate touring company which came to Dover. So there she is! It's as simple as that.'

'And what's she like?'

'You know her photographs. And you've seen her on the movies perhaps?'

'No. I don't think so. Is she very – what is the word? – very glamorous?'

'You're on the spot, farmer's wife and mother of five! She's glamorous. If she wasn't, she wouldn't be where she is. She's a brilliant actress, very gifted, and – now I come to think of it – very like her name: Louise Lafleur. Fantastic, as you said, Una – almost absurd!'

'You describe her rather – rather conventionally,' said Nell.

'Do I? Well, you see, a good actress is a convention, a thing made up of conventions. That's what she's paid to be.'

'Is she married?' Una enquired.

'Yes. To an actor. He's successful too. Adam Wolfe. You've surely seen *him* on the screen? His profile is famous.'

'Yes. I think so. I didn't like him much. Have they any children?'

'No.'

'You seem to know a lot about her,' said Nell.

'In theatrical circles we're maty and talkative. She knows a lot about this place, you know, and Croppy Boy and the brood mares.' He nodded towards the equine portraits, and laughed on a tone which he recognised as unwisely full of memories, but he lingered on the risk. He was remembering good fun and felt very lonely. 'Origins are often surprising, Una. You'd never think that Miss Lafleur was cradled in a banana crate. And I suppose you'd hardly think that I grew up on a stud farm. I don't look a bit horsy, do I? I wonder if she or I would be even faintly recognisable now to our ten-year-old selves?'

'She would, I imagine,' said Nell. 'She probably knew at ten exactly what she was going to be, and how she would look.'

Matt raised his brows. He was faintly irritated. 'Surely that's an extravagant shot,' he said. 'When you were ten did you know what you'd be, grownup?'

'I? Oh no.' She seemed surprised at his turning the attack on her, but she took it coolly. 'I don't suppose I thought at that age that I would eventually be History Mistress in the school where I was a pupil. But *I* didn't have fantastic dreams, or great strength of will.' She smiled with faint mischief but with an ease that banished all hint of bitterness from what she said. Yet his irritation remained.

'So she's a teacher,' he thought. 'A school marm. I might have known.' But why he might have known was not clear to him. Certainly her clothes did not give it away.

'Do you find it interesting – teaching history?' he asked coldly.

'Very.'

'Nell's an MA, if you please,' said Will and beamed at her, merely because he was aware of an unaccountable harshness in the atmosphere, and which seemed to threaten her. His nerves always flew to the rescue of discomfort, whether or not his mind could follow after. He was a very sensitive man.

Matt took the reproach of this vague, sweet bolstering up of a woman by no means in need of it and probably exasperated, but he could think of no phrase that was not comic with which to salute the announcement of her academic glory. He smiled therefore, conveying, he hoped the right degree of restrained *empressement.*

'Rubbish, this teaching,' said Una. 'Look at how thin this creature is! Quite unnecessary too.'

Nell's expression made it clear that she was used to this line of attack.

'If I didn't have this job, I couldn't have my car, or do half the things I like to do.'

'You could use Tom's car – he never wants it – and your own income is quite enough for your clothes and things.'

'And if Aunt Hannah turned me out one fine morning?'

'Time enough to worry when she does. But you know she adores you, really. Ah! Well – we've had this argument before!'

'We certainly have!'

'Una's on to her hobbyhorse, my dear,' said Will with great kindness to Nell. 'She'll never forgive you if you manage to dodge the slavery of marriage. She's jealous of your freedom!'

Everyone laughed.

'Do you hold with freedom for women, Matt? Do you think there's any point in it?' Una asked gaily.

'I hold with freedom for everyone. I think it's a terrific point! Personal liberty. Never was it so much in danger. Everyone is throwing in his hand about it. Everyone is asking to be put in clink.'

Una's eyes widened in amusement.

'But what nonsense you talk! With the whole world doing exactly as it chooses! Or so I understand from Will, when he puts down his paper every evening!'

'Yes, Matt,' said Will, 'there's been a little too much personal liberty everywhere, I'm thinking.'

'And soon there'll be none.'

'On the face of it that sounds like good news,' said Nell.

He stared at her.

'But what does this mean? Is de Valera as strong a brute as Mussolini then – or as Stalin?'

'Poor Dev. Indeed he isn't! Anyway Will and I always vote for Fine Gael.'

'I vote for Dev.' said Nell.

'And he's not so bad, either. I'm sometimes tempted to think that our poor old Cosgrave lot is done for.'

Will frowned at his wife. 'In God's name, Una, what do you know about it?'

'Nothing at all, dearest, I freely admit. But let's go and have coffee before the fight really starts.' She stood up.

The fight didn't start. As they crossed the hall they were greeted by shouts from the children, demanded to be visited. Liam, imperious and sweet in his pyjamas, stood at the head of the stairs and threatened to descent to the drawing room, so Una and Nell, gulped down their coffee and ran upstairs protesting.

Will said he'd look at the night, and Matt accompanied him. It was starry and aromatic.

'Ground frost,' said Will.

'Any harm in that?' asked the ignorant Matt.

'Not when it's as light as this.'

From the steps the river looked below them looked as if frozen, but its voice had gathered urgency in the night. So it had always done, Matt remembered. As a child he used to like to climb the big walnut tree, and now he recalled the nocturnal view from his perch up there, of the lamplit house, the polished surface of the river and the wide white curve of the weir. He could see his mother at her sewing in the drawing room; his father, burly in tailed tweed coat, cross the hall to tap the barometer, and come out on to the steps to look at the night, like Will. He could hear his father clear his throat and spit into the flowerbed. He could hear his fine, friendly voice – 'Where are you, Matt? Come down out of that tree, sir! Your mother's orders!' But Matt did not come down, and John Costello never troubled his head about being obeyed.

Life had taken urgency from the voice of the river on those nights. Dreams had been immense and every best potency assumed, and even felt, within the dreamer. Beauty had him by the heart then – but happily. In terms of shining nights and dewy mornings, river and fields and parental gentleness and schooldays' ease, young health and young hopes.

'"Ah, my childhood!"' he mocked himself. '"My pure, my happy childhood!"' And yet, it *had* been pure and happy. Why whimper about it then?

He shrugged. Sentimentality was natural on such an occasion as tonight – no need to wince at it. But he had come here in search of something other than nostalgia. He was in flight from the present, in pursuit of a future. Boyhood, telescoped into closeup for a minute by the night's circumstances, might have a passing smile and sigh, but it had no relevance to his dilemma. And yet – because he was tired today, he supposed – he knew himself disposed to cling to the obvious mood arising from this middle-aged return to the scene of childhood. It was a shield and a postponement. Escape from the particular to the general.

He walked across the meadow to the walnut tree, and took Will with him. Will was very like their father now. Taller, but not handsomer. A better businessman than John Costello, but hardly less generous and kind, Matt surmised. Happier – not needing to drink as their father sometimes did. Happier in marriage. Their mother had been very good to them but Matt suspected now, looking back, that as a wife she had been, perhaps, a little stern and grudging. But Will loved Una with the contentment of mastery.

'Can you smell the lilac?' Will asked.

'Yes. Same tree?'

'Same tree.'

Matt leant against the walnut trunk and stared into its branches.

'What time is it, Will?'

'About eight-thirty. Why?'

'No "why".'

Beginners, please. She was ready, in her first-act dress. Very still, her eyes completely emptied of reaction to things about her. Clouds of white muslin, faintly sprigged with pink. Like some nameless bird, fairer and more ethereal than a swan; like a new flower. Moss roses in her breast. Oh, summer's newborn self! Eyes, hands and mind brimful of the illusion now to be expressed. Oh, sweet interpreter, most tuneful instrument! Oh, heart of stone!

'Will, do you know, I've half a mind to climb this bloody old tree!'

But Will rarely found people ridiculous, and in many things was 'boy eternal.'

'Why don't you, in God's name?' he asked.

They strolled back to the house.

Una and Nell came downstairs together, calling back 'absolutely last' good nights to the still clamouring children. Una assumed a stern, bass tone.

'Be quiet, Liam. Go to sleep, sir!'

His faraway laugh was like a jet of light.

'Oh, Mother, I simply *love* it when you put on that voice! Good night, darling! Good night, Nell!'

Una shook her head as she opened the drawing room door.

'He's irrepressible, that child.'

'He's sweet.'

Una lighted the spirit flame under the retort of the coffee machine.

'Let's have some more coffee – in peace. There are cigarettes here – no, don't smoke your own.'

The two women sat on either side of the fire and smoked in silence for a minute. Nell leant back into the wing of her chair.

'You're looking a little tired,' Una said. 'And yet you're so nice with those exhausting kids! I often marvel at you.'

'Because I like Liam and Co?'

'Well, you get so many children all the week in your job –'

'Ah, but *these* children, Una!'

Una looked pleased. 'Here's your coffee. You spoil them. In a queer, off-hand sort of way, I admit – but still, you do spoil them.'

'I don't think so. Still – I find children easy – easier than grownups. I suppose it's because I'm a nasty, bossy character.'

'You're not bossy – only self-opinionated.' They both laughed. 'You didn't talk much at dinner, though you were asked on the understanding that you would.'

'I wasn't needed. You're more than a match for your brother-in-law, Una.'

'What do you think of him?'

'I? Oh, I don't know. If he had a paunch, he'd be Napoleon.'

'Really? Do you think he's like him? I've never noticed

it, but now you say it – Except that I always imagine Napoleon was very yellow-faced and Matt is as white as a sheet.'

'If he fattened up, you'd see it better. Yes, more coffee, please.'

'He's not so *very* thin –'

'No. He has the jowl already. Perhaps by the time he's fifty, he'll be able to go on the halls or the movies or something.'

'He won't need to. I think he's making quite a lot of money nowadays.'

'Why has he honoured you with this sudden visit?'

'He hasn't said yet. As you know, Will had a wire from him on Tuesday, asking if he might come. We wired back, and he wired again to say he'd be here this morning. Will is enchanted, of course. And I must say I like the idea of having him round and showing him off. I always find him awfully nice and easy.'

'Pity he wouldn't be! You don't imagine he ought to be superior, do you?'

'I might be surprised if he were – but still, people get conceited, you know. They can't help it. I wonder why he doesn't marry. Would you say he looks unhappy, Nell?'

'I haven't noticed.'

Will and Matt came into the room.

'Law and order restored upstairs?'

'After a fashion. Are your ears red, Matt?'

'Ah, so he's been getting the once-over?'

'Naturally. Nell says that if you had a – a tummy, you'd be Napoleon.'

'People have said that before.' (You're not the first to say it, Louise. But it's always been women. He could hear her appreciative laugh). 'But it isn't as easy as just putting on flesh, you know. Napoleon was five-foot-two, I think?'

'Oh, we're not pretending that you aren't a much finer man than the Emperor!' said Una. 'Only you're just a little like him, that's all.'

'And the stray lock of hair is quite accidental?' said Nell.

Matt became very bland to conceal irritation. This young woman's sarcasm bored him. How much better off would she be with Una's sweet impudence!

'Actually, quite accidental. My hair is not at all like Napoleon's, which seems to have been thin and weak.' He smiled at Una, with whom he felt safe and even gay. 'Mine is a pest, it grows so thick and untidy. Indeed, I sometimes think that this awful mop is the only sign left now that I too went to jail for Cathleen Ni Houlihan!'

'Do you object to there being even that sign left?'

'Not in the least, Miss – Miss Nell.'

'Oh Lord, call her "Nell"!' said Will. 'Why, you're practically brother and sister.'

Matt and Nell smiled vaguely at each other in acceptance of this dim relationship.

'Actually, your hair *is* rather like an IRA man's,' said Una. 'Are they afraid of you in London?'

'Not so very, mind you! But they sometimes put on Irish accents to placate me. And the really maty ones call me Pat.'

'Oh dear! But they're nice people, the English. Don't you think so?'

'Emphatically. Much nicer than us. They have much better manners, for one thing – London has certainly been mighty civil to this ex-gunman!'

'Have we got bad manners?' Nell asked him.

He tackled her, looking straight into her grey eyes. He assumed a faintly wheedling and confidential tone in the hope that it might take the ring of effrontery out of a personal assault.

'You talk with such curious detachment,' he said, 'that

it's impossible not to suspect you of leg pulling.'

'Oh, and maybe you're right,' said Will, whose kindly notion it always was to back up the women and make mysteries out of them. But Matt, keeping his eye on Nell, thought he saw her shrink further into the shelter of her chair.

'I don't leg pull,' she said. 'I'm not at all humorous.'

He dropped it. She was impossible. And yet he admitted that she looked both touching and distinguished as she spoke. He could only smile apologetically and cross to where Una sat on the sofa.

'She's quite humorous, as a matter of fact,' said the latter, making room for him beside her on the sofa. 'Liam is always quoting her jokes.'

Will had been rooting in the bottom of a cabinet.

'There are a lot of snapshots here,' he said. 'They might amuse you, Matt. Some of the old ones are interesting.' He laid an armful of albums on the sofa.

'Some of the recent ones need pasting up,' said Una. 'I really ought to do them.'

'I wish you would, my dear.'

Matt was feeling restless and depressed – unequal to snapshot albums – but he tackled one of them. It was a very old one, filled with curious little yellowing pictures from 1910–1912. He had won prizes in the *Boy's Own Paper* with his Brownie No. 2 photographs. Here they were, some of the prizewinners. Linda and Jim digging castles on the strand at Kilbeggan. Dear Linda – she looked a gay enough kid. It was a good snap.

'Will, darling – why don't you sing something for Matt?'

Will looked pleased and shy. Matt remembered then how he had always liked to sing.

'Do, Will – there's a good chap.'

'Oh no!'

'Yes, go on. Don't be silly.'

'Nell, will you play for him?'

'Oh, Una – can't you?'

'No, not tonight. I'm tired. I'd like to listen.'

'All right, then.' She stood up. She was quite amazingly graceful, Matt conceded.

Will sang, and once started went on singing. He had a tuneful light baritone voice, and it gave him real, though quite modest, pleasure to use it. Requiring only absent-minded 'thank you's' and 'what nexts' from the sofa, he went from song to song. All the tunes were familiar to Matt. Mainly they were the sentimental drawing room ballads which his father and mother had sung in pre-war years.

It was easy to look at old photographs and listen to Will. She plays well, he thought, and she looks quite beautiful at the piano.

'Do you mind if I skim through "The Irishman's Diary"?' Una asked him softly, picking up *The Irish Times*. 'I always like him – he's nice and gossipy.'

'Not at all. But is that how you listen to your husband's singing?'

'Oh, I can do both. And if I get him singing I have a chance of the paper for a few minutes in peace. He fusses when I'm reading it – says I muddle it up.'

She chuckled with guilty pleasure. Will was warbling innocently about 'When I gaze in beauty's eyes.' Beauty's eyes! Matt winced, and returned to the photographs.

He was the third child of his parents, who had had seven children. Will, who was the eldest, and forty now, had gone to France with the Munster Fusiliers when he left school in 1915; nine months later Joe, the second member of the family, had followed him there. Both had done well in the war, and in the week before the armistice Joe was killed. Matt left school in 1918 and went to University

College, Dublin, hoping to obtain some sort of Bachelor of Arts degree, and with the intention of conquering the world of literature, or journalism. In Dublin he became poetic and wild. Also he joined the IRA. He fought against the Black and Tans through the winter of 1920–21, and in the following spring went to prison. After the truce and the Treaty, believing Michael Collins to be right and de Valera wrong, but having no heart for civil war, no money and no Bachelor of Arts degree, he left Ireland, went to Paris and got a miserable tutoring job. Thereafter his life had been the usual struggle – into eventual ease – of the literary man. He was now, in worldly terms, the most successful member of the family. And after him came Will, he supposed. The younger ones had not had so much luck. Their parents dying when they were still unfledged, their mother during the war and their father, depressed and in debt, in 1920, they had had to jump off into life with almost no money, and with only foolish and fussy counsel from aunts and lawyers. Linda, lovely Linda, who simply could *not* learn shorthand and who nearly died of boredom being a governess in Dalkey, married a stray American whom she met on Kingstown Pier – and now, deserted by him, bitter, hard and ill, with three children to look after, lived in Cincinnati, supported by Matt, and refused to come home. Will kept up a pointless correspondence with her. Matt often thought of her, but rarely wrote, leaving her affairs to his lawyer. Linda had been wasted certainly – had wasted herself – but what was there to do? She probably had some reason of the heart, perhaps the reason of faithful waiting, which kept her whimpering in Cincinnati. Jimmy was a Jesuit in Melbourne – happy and safe, it might be assumed. Peg, unmarried, was now the secretary of a magnate in Chicago. Her letters were smart and hard. She paddled her own canoe, but Matt knew that Will worried about her, and suspected her of living what he called an immoral life.

Dolly, the youngest, tiresome in the nursery, was tiresome now – and unlucky. Married to a bank clerk stationed in County Roscommon, she was always in trouble. Her husband was an ass; drank and got into muddles with bookies, and sometimes had narrow shaves of public scandal with girls. Dolly's children had bad health, and so had Dolly. And she was a quarreller, and nothing that was ever arranged for her was right. Although Matt and Will always produced whatever money was required for her crises, she had long ago ceased to be on correspondence terms with the former, to his great relief – but compensatorily she gave Will a great deal of annoyance.

That was the family which he found now, gay, challenging and babyish, in the Brownie snapshots. Well, he thought, a pretty average shakeout. A rather normal family history. Not so ghastly as some. Funny though that he should have been the luckiest one. He, who tonight accounted himself so deeply unlucky. He, who *was* unlucky.

'I'm thankful Dolly won't know me anymore,' he whispered to Una. (Will was singing the pianissimo last verse of 'She is Far From the Land.') 'It would be a fearful bore if I had to go up to Roscommon to see her.'

'Oh, Dolly! I could strangle the creature,' said Una. 'Have you seen *Romeo and Juliet* on the film? I see it's going to be in Dublin soon. I like Shearer.'

So the evening passed. Clear enough in itself, but to Matt unreal-seeming in that it was, by his deliberate choice, doing service as a screen. And as the light of oil lamps in this drawing room gave novel, because long-forgotten, values to faces and objects – curiously making one accept them both more subjectively and more guardedly than was habitual – so from this place, from this forgotten lighting the too long familiar, the too insufferably dear, imperative and exigent would probably grow impressionistic and escapable.

He wondered at what time they went to bed. Early, he imagined, on a farm. He dreaded early hours, being a bad sleeper and one in whom the silence of a sleeping house could sometimes create a kind of frenzied sorrow. Well, he had many new books in his room, hundreds of cigarettes, and the river's new-old voice would break the anguish of stillness. He would be alone too, alone. He could drop the screen and turn back – ah, yes, this last, last time – into reality. Forbidden country from which at length he had found courage to flee, and to which, whilst here, whilst seeking a substitute, he was not to return in fantasy. Ah, but tonight, the first night. You ask the impossible, Louise. Always – that is your gift.

No, he hoped they would not go to bed too early. It was easier down here. He lighted another cigarette.

'You've been clever with this room, Una. You've made it very charming without destroying its associative character.'

'It's an easy room to make attractive, don't you think?'

'Yes. I always loved those three long windows.'

It was a pretty scene – tranquil and traditional, modestly civilised. Looking at it, living in it, one might be permitted to doubt whether the world of one's childhood, re-enacting itself here so confidently, was, in fact, for all the thoughtful world, a thing of ruins and archaisms. Chains clanking; bombers roaring through the once free sky; scholarship and art in prison or in the pay of politicians' ideologies; imperialism, bankrupt notion, falsely inflated everywhere; nationalisms foaming at the mouth; grown men taking instruction from this little creature or that as to how they shall think; how, or if, they shall pray; how they are to breed, what work they may do, how many rooms they may occupy; what salute they must give to what flag, and what songs they must sing. Abyssinia, China, Spain. Spain – one of Europe's eternal glories – tearing herself apart, being helped to do it, not being hindered. The same doom awaiting every country in every other country's rearmament intentions. Man's courageous, individual heart undiscoverable anywhere. Even at last the poets in vocal flight – to absurd and terrible obedience. Hugging their chains. Singing the new theme of captivity. Yet here around him this pretty scene of ease and natural hope, this sample of continuity. In a dictator's country too. But a more subtle dictator than most – though he also, given time, might have the minds of his people in chains. He did not bring materialism out for public adoration, but materialistic justice controlled by a dangerous moral philosophy, the new Calvinism of the Roman Catholic. That was his rod, his particular bundle of fasces. He used it subtly, but the Church, having less reason than he to walk with care, did not so trouble. And now the proffered Constitution of the Irish Free State was before the world. Founded, intelligibly enough and even as this house was, upon the family as social unit, and upon the controlled but inalienable rights of private ownership, but offering in its text curious anomalies and subtleties, alarming signposts. Dedicated to the Holy Trinity – why not the Holy Family? – but much more in step with the times than was apparent to such men as Will, for instance. Subtle, but dictatorial and obstinate. Quite up-to-date, if more discreet than smart-seeming. A clever man, Dev. Indeed, a statesman – but twentieth century. Well, the Free State would vote on its Constitution, and Matt imagined, and imagined that de Valera too imagined, that Ireland, newly patrolled by the Church, would be unlikely to vote solid against the Holy Trinity. Certainly this household wouldn't, whatever it might think of Dev.

There is no escape for a man from his own time, Matt reflected wearily, save in his own nature – in his use of memory and imagination. By these, by his unconscious reliance on them, Will for instance held this illusive oasis.

He created his present out of what he knew and wanted – and was happy, and good, in a sad and evil world. That was something – that was decidedly a contribution, a courageous one. There were many men like Will. There could be many more – even under Dev's tricky constitution. Perhaps they were the innocent hope of the world.

'You're looking very sad, Matt. You have a sad sort of face.'

'Have I?'

'Why don't you get married?'

'Find me a wife.'

'I wouldn't dare. You'd be hard to please.'

Will was singing 'Who is Sylvia?' Singing it well. Matt closed his eyes and listened with attention, with a kind of gratitude. The song flew to its end, as it should. It should be quick as a summer wind, or a courting swallow. '... She excels each mortal thing upon the dull earth dwelling ...' Oh God, oh God, for words like that to praise her!

The song ended, and Matt opened his eyes and looked towards the two performers, met Nell's which happened to be upon him.

She closed the piano.

'That's enough for tonight,' said Will. 'Are you deaf from us, the two of you?'

'Nothing of the kind. It was fine.'

'Thank you, Will dearest. You're in great form.'

Una went to a side table where there was a silver tray with drinks.

'Glass of milk, Nell?'

'No, thanks, Una.'

'Oh, but it would be good for you. Our famous milk?'

'Whiskey for you, Matt?' said Will. 'No use offering you the wine of the country, I'm afraid.'

'But I thought Jameson, or Guinness, was that?'

'Not nowadays. We dairy farmers are a power in the land now, my boy.'

He brought Matt his whiskey, and drank milk himself.

'Here's long life to *The Heart of Stone*,' he said.

Una yawned a little, sipping her milk. Nell said she must go home. They all strolled out on to the steps with her. The sky was full of stars and the river looked brilliant.

'Tomorrow in Quinlan's field – about four. Tell Tom he's got to come. Do you hear?'

'All right, Una. Good night. Good night, everybody.'

She got into her car and started the engine.

'Good night, Nell. Safe home.'

They strolled back to the drawing room and finished their drinks. Will, yawning expansively, fastened the window catches. Matt stood up and said good night. Una looked sympathetic.

'You must be dying for a proper night in bed, after that journey. Sleep like the dead.'

'I will. Good night, both of you.'

He took a silver candlestick from the hall and went upstairs light-footedly to the room he had shared through boyhood with his brother Jimmy. How familiar the journey seemed even now! A clock struck eleven somewhere. She was taking her curtains. How many tonight? Tall, laughing, trembling, happy. Herself again, released from inspiration. '... To her garlands let us bring!' He sang it out suddenly, in a gust of delight. Then he remembered the houseful of sleeping children. He stole into his room, feeling cold and homesick.

The Second Chapter

'I'm not a Wordsworthian, Matt,' said Tom Mahoney. 'The sounding cataract has never haunted me like a passion. Passions, on the other hand, have sometimes haunted me like sounding cataracts.'

Matt smiled, and, glancing at Nell, saw that she smiled too. She seemed at ease, relaxed. She leant back from the steering wheel and the car ran unnecessarily fast, Matt thought, under her casual-seeming touch. She wore no hat, and the breeze lifted her hair. There was a very faint flush in her cheeks.

The three were driving back to Mellick from the lake. Tom, sprawling diagonally across the back of the car. He had insisted that Matt should dine with him.

'My mother will be disgusted. She isn't hospitable, even to the clergy, and she believes you to be a wholly immoral man. But it's my house as much as hers. Pay no attention to her.'

'But this afternoon wasn't Wordsworthian,' said Matt now. 'He didn't go on picnics.'

'How do you know? He married, didn't he? And in

youth he had a "family outing" all right. To Calais Beach. "Dear child, dear girl, that walkest with me here!"' Tom laughed to himself.

Matt thought this a racy remark to make in Irish society, and did not look at Nell. He assumed that Tom Mahoney had established a right to certain privileges of speech.

'Nature,' the latter continued from the back of the car, 'what that old Romantic meant by Nature, is only raw material, only a germ for the imagination. And you could master it all, for your purely imaginative purposes, by deduction from your first daisy chain. No man of poetic parts needs to be puddling round indefinitely with an external suggestion. I'm speaking of your type, Matt – the imaginative-emotional-creative. Only in a very secondary sense intellectual. For myself, "Lake-poet" Nature isn't even a germ. Does nothing to me. I'm not a poet, of course. I am a moral philosopher. Man is my animal and I like to sit in the field where he habitually grazes. I've never found a readable book in a running brook.'

'Then the picnic bored you?' Nell asked.

'Not at all, Nell. Because by God's mercy I wasn't picnicking by myself. And your sister, my cousin Una – well, she's very nearly my favourite study.'

'Why?'

'Happiness, Matt. Happiness, you novelist, you! Happiness as innocent as our picnic. Have you ever seen it before, Matt? Will you ever see it again? If I were a novelist, I'd write a Victorian three-decker all about Una. And it wouldn't be censored either! It wouldn't as much as bring a blush to my mother's ageing cheek!'

Nell laughed softly and took a corner very fast.

'Of course, nature's only a suggestion,' said Matt. 'But we get tired and fuddled, we lose the urgency of idea, and the suggestion is good and perpetual. We have to return, for some reason, to have a look at it.'

'I think that the less a man gazes at his spring ideas, the better. He has to start from somewhere – ok. But these circular tours!'

'Look in your heart and write?' asked Nell.

'"Heart" is a suspect word, but it's a better idea than peering too closely at "Meadow, grove and stream." Nell, will you mind your driving? You may possibly have a genius in the car.'

'In which seat, Tom?'

'In front, on your left. The man of imagination. Imagination, although Plato reckons it the fourth faculty of the soul, is, all the same, other things being equal, the final essential of genius. Many men of imagination are fools, I admit, but I really think there's never been a genius without it. And Matt has it, and he's not a fool, and some of his reviewers have called him a genius – so, just in case, Nell – mind where you're driving!'

'The advantage of looking in your heart to write,' said Matt, 'is that you actually see nothing.'

'Precisely. You just have to invent – which is your function.'

'You're both surprising me,' said Nell. 'Or is it just that I'm stupid?'

'You're not stupid,' said Tom. 'It's a pity you aren't. If you'd only decide to be as stupid as your sister – and that's not idiot-standard – you might be as happy as she is. And I'd write two three-deckers!'

'Well, I'll think it over when I've read the first, Tom. I'll see if I like what you present as happiness.'

'You won't.'

Matt thought that she looked today as if she could on occasion be very happy.

'You've enjoyed the afternoon?' he ventured politely.

'Oh, I love the lake. The others will be there for ages yet. Will and Liam anyway.' She sounded quite simply wistful.

'How will they get home?' Tom asked.

'They'll get a lift from some other fisherman, or Una will drive back for them after dinner, perhaps.'

'You're very busy chauffeurs, you and Una,' Matt observed.

'Yes, we're always victimised for it. Now, for instance, if Tom weren't so determined to eat at his usual hour, *or* if he'd use his own car, I could still be on the lake. Do you hear, Tom?'

'I do. You'd be catching cold – or getting bitten all over by those damned old mayfly.'

'They don't bite.'

'Well, they tickle. Themselves and their nuptial dance!'

'They're lovely creatures,' Nell persisted.

'Ephemeridae,' said Matt. 'Six hours of life, I believe, Tom – but said to be flawless. How would you like it?'

'Who says it's flawless?'

'Well, years maybe as a slimy river larva; then the hour strikes and you rise and shed your shell on the surface of a summery lake; you are suddenly perfectly beautiful, and surrounded by hundreds of your species, just as beautiful. The sun shines, you dance a love dance all through the evening, you propagate your species, and without eating or drinking or being anyway gross you die on the shadowy waters.'

'I don't see how you can propagate your species without being any way gross,' said Tom. 'Or if you can, it seems a damn shame.'

The lady and gentleman in the front of the car allowed that remark to fall into silence.

The drive from the lake to Mellick was nearly forty miles, and through beautiful country which for long had been Matt's whole world. As it slid past him now, water and wood and blue hills, he was surprised at how automatically the names of landmarks rose to his mind.

It was an evening of great beauty – the second last day of May. The lake, narrowing to become a river again, reflected the last light dazzlingly, so that the wooded slopes on its eastern shore were dramatised into near-blackness, as were its many islands. But the sky was gentle nevertheless, even in the now expectant west; the day was ending graciously, without unnecessary theatre, as he had seen it end a thousand times above these hills.

'Do you remember in Dublin, Matt, I used to call you the Minstrel Boy? Faith, you weren't long about losing the wild harp. Dropped it overboard when Dunleary faded from view, I'm thinking.'

'It was an awkward instrument – and damn monotonous.'

'You're right there. Since then you've been trying to learn to play a Stradivarius, I think. But you were a great boyo all the same in those simple days. The hell of a ladykiller too!'

'I was nothing of the kind. That's a mean, low-down thing to say. As I remember it you were the *caballero.*'

'Oh, in a crude way. I had my – ahem! – realistic triumphs. But your method was much more effective. Give you your due, I don't think you were entirely aware of your success. But I can see you now stalking through Stephen's Green – looking as shabby as hell, no hat on you, and the lock of hair falling into the visionary's blue eye. Ah, those poor young ladies in First Arts!'

'I wish I'd been up in your years,' said Nell. 'It would have been marvellous to have seen the two of you giving the girls a treat.'

'We did that all right, Nell – believe it or not. But Matt worked on a higher plane of appeal than I, though I'm now a respectable citizen, and he is what you see. In those days death for Ireland, glorious young death, was stamped all over his face. That was the mood we were in –

especially the girls.'

'Well, it was an effective mood,' said Nell severely. 'It accomplished a lot.'

'Certainly it did. And here you have two of its forgotten heroes.'

'I wish I could think that all its forgotten heroes were as prosperous and pleased with themselves.' She laughed sideways at Matt. She had a curious way of refusing to let one be offended by her snubs.

'I echo your pious wish,' he responded demurely. 'And it wasn't I who grumbled, you know.'

'Oh, I don't want my statue put up *yet,*' said Tom. 'Patriotism is not enough. Wait awhile. Wait until the Mayor and Corporation of Mellick, or more likely, the Men's Confraternity, have doled me out the hemlock.'

'But I thought you said you were a respectable citizen?'

'Only by a charitable fiction which may break down at any minute. Or because I live with my mother, perhaps.'

Mellick was in sight now, across the rivered plain. Grey and gentle, beautifully spired. Its long-forgotten look of venerable composure took Matt with sudden pleasure and surprise.

'What a lovely town it is!' he said.

Nell gave him a quick, pleased look.

'They're doing their best to spoil it,' she said, 'but it's still lovely from here.'

'The roofs of a town are always a pleasant sight,' said Tom. 'But look here, Matt, about this Wordsworthian weakness. Keats found his poetry under his own hat. He didn't interview Nature – he invented her when he felt the call.'

'Yes. And the Elizabethans too. They were city chaps – pubcrawlers.'

'You're right. But Keats now – a little Cockney from Walthamstow – when was he left alone with a sounding cataract, will you tell me?'

'He went to Scotland,' said Nell, 'and the Isle of Wight and –'

'Aye – and to Italy when it was too late. But none of it impressed him like his own inventions. Do you remember, Matt, a good remark he made in apology for not being enchanted by some little bit of scenery? He thought that perhaps if –'

'Yes,' said Matt. He remembered the remark. Perhaps if it had taken my Cockney maidenhead. He would prefer that it was not boomed from the back of the car at this moment. 'For a moral philosopher, you waste a lot of time memorising this and that about the poets.'

'I don't memorise. I'm cursed with a mind that retains irrelevant rubbish. That's why I do well as a lawyer.'

The straggling old town was coming out to meet them now, not noticeably extended or improved since Matt had been used to cycle into it to school along this road. A better road surface, an occasional petrol station, some new, clean cottages – but still the town of childhood.

Boys played football all over the wide road.

'These wretched children,' said Nell. 'And in the Sunday traffic, too!'

Matt smiled at the Sunday traffic.

'This is Lotus Land,' he said. 'You are all dreamers here.'

She smiled at him.

'That's the sort of remark we don't like from visitors,' she said.

'Then the more fools you,' he retorted, 'and anyhow, I'm not a visitor.'

Dinner passed off smoothly in the big, Georgian house in

King Street. Aunt Hannah, Mrs. Thomas Mahoney, was magnificently unwelcoming to Matt, and pointed out a number of reasons why it would have been more comfortable and suitable for him to have dined at Weir House. Tom said nothing during these speeches; merely handed Matt a glass of whiskey. His mother eyed it.

'That's far too strong, Tom. Do you want to kill him? You ought to consider other people's tastes, you know. Well, now you're here we might as well dine.'

She swept across the lofty drawing room and her guest opened the door for her.

She was a beautifully made woman, and walked as if she knew it. She had white hair, and was picturesquely dressed in amethyst foulard, with a jingling chatelaine, and a silver spectacle case hanging from her belt.

The food was good, but Mrs. Mahoney did not urge it upon anyone. She ate well herself and was imperious with the servants. The dining room in which they sat was on the first floor, behind the drawing room. Tom's offices occupied the ground floor, and obviously the kitchen and servants' quarters must be in the basement. There was no service lift, yet dinner proceeded without a hitch in a prosperous Victorian setting. Matt marvelled. Continuity indeed! Was it still possible to ask your fellow creatures to race up and down four flights of stairs with your roast lamb and green peas?

He also marvelled at the strength of the three personalities which shared the benefits of this archaic and smooth routine, and which yet kept so far apart from each other, were so pointedly and eccentrically themselves.

Nell seemed not as much in awe of her aunt as Tom pretended to be of his mother. Merely bored, and concealing, she hoped, her boredom from the visitor. She disagreed with Aunt Hannah as coolly as she might with anyone else, and betrayed none of the solicitude which young women sometimes give to old. Tom ate and drank, and talked rather less than seemed natural, but Matt felt that this too was merely from mild boredom, and a male habit of letting the old lady have her illusion of herself. Mrs. Mahoney did most of the talking. She told Matt that his literary work was a disgrace to Ireland, and that she had never read a word of it, she was happy to say. She wondered what brought him to Mellick now, and assumed he wouldn't stay very long. She deplored Una's method of bringing up children and said that Liam's character was ruined beyond repair. She expected they had had an uncomfortable afternoon by the lake, and she decided that Leahy, her butcher, was cheating again, that this undoubtedly was Canterbury lamb, and she certainly could not recommend Matt to have any more of it.

Matt raised his brows to all this and said 'Yes?' and 'No?' But there was no conversation, and the meal was eaten in an atmosphere from which all feeling was, as it were, naturally eliminated. Matt thought that probably both Tom and Nell were too grownup and self-sufficient to bother to pit real life against such an unreality as this old lady.

There was coffee in the drawing room, and a lecture from Mrs. Mahoney to Tom about the number of lights he switched on.

'Come on downstairs,' said Tom to Matt. 'I want to talk to you. Good night, Mother.'

'Don't be late, Tom. How will your visitor get home tonight?'

'I'll telephone Gallagher to send a driver with my car when I want it. Good night, Nell.'

The men bowed themselves out of the big drawing room. Matt, looking back from the door, saw Nell lean forward from a sofa to pick up a book, and thought that she looked far too beautiful for the deadly evening ahead of her.

Tom used his inner office as a study. It was a tall, pleasant room with one long window. Although overfilled with books, both legal and general, it was orderly and comfortable. There were green leather armchairs on either side of a Georgian mantelpiece. Tom put decanters and cigars on the mahogany table desk.

'Funny to meet again as ageing clubmen,' he said.

'You haven't changed much,' said Matt. Tom had always been a heavy-shouldered and rather fleshy giant, his eyes had always been half shut and very quick, his fairish hair had always receded from his temples. He had always looked lazy, well-dressed and imperturbable.

'The change in you is marked,' he said now to Matt.

'I've learnt to be neat and tidy.'

'Yes. To keep things in their places – your heart in your boots, for instance. It used to rampage on your sleeve.'

'We were young, my dear chap.'

'And expected to be happier fellows when we should be middle-aged.'

'Aren't you?'

'Don't I look it? I never aimed at the bliss of such as your brother Will. But you're miserable. Here, have a drink.'

They drank, and lighted cigars.

'It's a miserable world,' Matt ventured. 'It always was.'

'But we didn't know it. Or we thought that we would change all that. Instead we've made it worse – all of us.'

'This cosmic conscience!'

'You find me naïve?'

'Like the "Skibbereen Eagle". But if you think you're going to get away with the world situation as a reason for bittersweetness –'

'For a writer it's good personal reason for bitterness – I swear it. What are we to do? How can we escape from our own time? Tell me, in fact, Tom, what civilisation is in the end? Is it an affair of mechanical administration, an affair of State, or is it what we used to think – the spontaneous gift of individual minds, the impeccable, free thing that only unconsciously and accidentally conditions administration?'

'I'll try to answer you out of Plato, if you like – and you know how he suspected your kind of gentry. But leave me alone with your rhetoric. Your personal life will last your own time, man! Enjoy it – and amuse us with your Stradivarius. No one's asking more than that of you!'

Matt looked like a man who flings aside a thousand angry answers. Then he laughed.

'Forgive me, Tom,' he said. 'Upon my soul, you seem to be making me feel young.'

'Not young enough to play the Prince of Denmark, let us hope. What's brought you running home like this?'

'Good God! Why should I not come home?'

'Above in that field this afternoon I took a good look at you, my boyo. Your career has interested me – so I gave you the once-over, for the instruction of my Socratic soul. And do you know all that came into my head? "Man delights him not nor woman neither, Stephen said. He returns after a life of absence to that spot of earth where he was born, where he has always been, man and boy, a silent witness and then, his journey of life ended, he plants his mulberry tree in the earth. Then dies. The motion is ended. Gravediggers bury Hamlet *père* and Hamlet *fils.* A king and a prince at last in death –"'

'Do you know *Ulysses* by heart?'

'No. But I know that conversation in the library. The best conversation Ireland has done yet.'

'I'm not the Bard – and there is no Anne Hathaway here – what is it? "And in New Place a slack, dishonoured body that once was comely –"

'The mobled queen – stretched back in the second-best bed! No such cosiness for you – that's a fact. So what are you here for? Is it time to plant the mulberry tree?'

'I don't take myself as bloody seriously as you imagine.'

'Oh yes, you do. We all take ourselves more seriously than anyone else could possibly imagine. But it's dull – your returning a mask. I was expecting a devil of a fellow – and to have the grosser parts of my education increased magnificently by meeting you again – a sophisticated dog. You were well endowed for the personal life, you always went at it pluckily enough – and your work has the ring of knowledge now. And, my God, here you turn up at thirty-seven, successful, not to say eminent – travelled, cosseted, experienced – and all you have to show for it is a civil expression of countenance, and the lovely manners of a Jesuit!'

Matt closed his eyes. Is it time to plant the mulberry tree? Oh, barrenness. Is it not enough to be in flight? The positive strength required for that makes it almost seem creative. But there whence he fled was the seed. There in that face, where roses and soft lilies blow, he had found at his most emptied moment a personal answer to contemporary negation; found that which he had long ceased to look for. And found it good and durable. His seed, his potency. In every hour with her there was vitality, and a forgetfulness of the immediate and the topical that made the writer flame with arrogant courage. No former love of his had ever thus fed talent – but rather had been withheld from tampering with it; a recreation, love, a reassurance. Never before an exaction of that part of him he held most guardedly and deeply precious – his work, which always he had fed in private, on dreams and guesses. He had wanted a wife always, but never found where he could have the one he wanted. He had not thought that in his day a man looked for, or found, a Muse. Then she had come, and filling him with pleasure as with noonday light, had made him master again in the nick of time of his life and his ideas, had made him deaf to contemporary theorists and ideologists, had reasserted values which he had desired to find eternal, but which in his day were held for dead and evil. Into her radiant myth he had escaped from the weight and dogmatism of his time; had found his own conceptions – in every hour with her a new one. He had been amazed – but so it was. She asserted personal vision. She was – and how it had delighted her! – his Muse.

He remembered telling her the names of the Muses. She knew only a few things, having had no education, and an adult life for the most part of sharp struggle. Yet suddenly she would flash out an accurate and unlooked-for piece of knowledge. She had a flair, which derived from her own great talent, for whatever was poetic, vivid or moving. She knew the ring of good words, and a true line from a false. She knew – to a nicety that was almost suspect – the value of simplicity and non-pretentiousness. She never faked, or tried for what she was not. On the other hand, she often gave off-stage – she couldn't help it – magnificent performances of herself. 'But so do you, my darling,' she would say amusedly to that. 'You play the tormented author so beautifully, Matt, that I'm sure you'd have been a good actor.'

It was exactly two years now since they had met – at a cocktail party in Chester Square. A brilliant afternoon towards the end of May. Fighting his way on to the balcony for a breath of air, he had found her and had fallen into talk with her. Exchanging names, each gravely acknowledged the renown of the other, but he admitted that he had never seen her act, and she had neither read his famous novels nor attended any of his three unlucky plays.

She was then in the first flush of absolute success. He had been abroad all the winter and had not seen those acclaimed Shakespearean performances at the Old Vic which had brought her with the spring to Shaftesbury Avenue and to perfect triumph in the leading part of a fabulously successful modern comedy. And standing now in the sun, her hat wreathed with tiny roses, her dress a pinkish cloud, blue-eyed, white-skinned and smiling, she looked, the playwright thought, exactly everything that the world desires its leading actresses to be. She looked the perfect exponent of that illusion for which men are said to have died, and without which their hearts shrivel.

He was amused at meeting such a fairytale. They grew confidential. She told him of childhood in Dover – not yet of the greengrocer's shop – of how religious Huguenots are, of her first tour, and her first London chance. 'I was the little, sobbing tart,' she said. 'You know the part – four lines. It's everyone's first London chance. And the play always runs five nights. That one did.' He told her about Weir House, and bicycling to school, about Dublin and the Black and Tans and going to prison. She was impressed by his having been in prison. 'And now here we are, famous people, drinking champagne cocktails in – in Belgravia, isn't it?' she had said as they lifted their glasses to their triumphs, smiling at each other. Before he left the party, he had met Adam Wolfe, her husband, blond, amiable giant with a handsome face which was vaguely familiar – probably from the screen. That night, obtaining a stall with difficulty, he had gone to her play. The next day he sent roses and a note:

> I was at the play last night. I shall be there again tonight – indeed I foresee that unless I watch myself I shall be there every night of the run. May I come to your dressing room tonight to thank you for your matchless performance? And, if you have nothing else to do, will you have supper with me?
>
> MATT COSTELLO

A prelude like many others he had played – but he had known that here was no stale adventure in repetition. She had had supper with him, and thereafter life was re-made. The desert blossomed like the rose.

'It's a woman, of course. But surely this isn't the first one to make you run for cover? Running this direction though – that gives me pause. When the addicted wanderer makes for home –'

'I'm tired, I tell you, man! I'm sick of town, and there's no quiet left in England. I wanted to see Will's kids – and to find out what Dev is really doing for Cathleen Ni Houlihan's four green fields! How dated that phrase is, Tom! How old it makes us!'

'No older than we are. Then you're not talking? But there *is* a woman over there? You *are* in love?'

Matt was surprised by the manner of these questions. They were curiously deliberate.

'Keep County Court tactics out of this,' he said good-naturedly. 'I'm none of your perjuring farmers.'

'I wish to God you were – then I'd know how to make you answer straight, you twister. But the fact that you don't answer is enough. You're in love, you poor fool.'

Matt saw that the other man intended to have an answer and that therefore his best blockade was frankness.

'Yes,' he said with a cunning smile of surrender. 'Yes, I'm in love. It's a habit of mine.'

He was again surprised at the repressed explosiveness of the laugh with which Tom – wily lawyer – took his bit of comedy-playing. Evidently he had said what gave satisfaction, and he was believed. His host refilled the glasses.

'Then you won't be staying amongst us?' he said, and Matt could not exactly qualify the intonation of the query. 'You're not going to settle down and live decent, I mean? We have lots of smiling virgins, you know, whose mothers wouldn't mind –'

'Oh, don't be so sure! I write indecent books and I don't

go to Mass on Sunday.'

'Ah – a lot of that could be glossed over. You're rich and famous, and you come of well-respected people. Weren't you born and bred here, God help you, child – and all your people before you? And what's all that you get on with but a lot of foolishness? You'd soon grow out of it. Not at all, Mr. Costello – no obstacle at all. A nice young wife now is the very thing for you. "Let copulation thrive." And before you can remember your last mortal sin you'll be going to Confession every Saturday.'

'Like you?'

'Like me when I marry.'

'And when will that be?'

'When there's figs on thistles.'

'You used to be – more appreciative of the sex.'

'There is a brothel in the town, in the town,' sang Tom.

'In Mellick?'

'Two, I believe. But the outsides are a fine, symbolic warning. Anyway a poor chap I know was seen going into one of them on a certain Wednesday night, and on Friday when he got his wages he got the sack. I tell you, sir, this city is going to be run on decent lines, or we're all going to know the reason why. Did you think you'd come to the land of the free?'

'I didn't. But you seem free enough – in your talk anyway.'

'Within these four walls. But I live with a couple of the female pillars of Mellick, my boy!' He waved a hand towards the ceiling.

'One of them stands a good deal from you,' said Matt.

'You mean Nell? Oh, that's a sort of game we play – I try to make her snarl at me, and she shows me she's paying no attention at all. I'm some parts of a gentleman, and so I let her win. I could easily win though – I could make a joke or two for the benefit of that light of the Legion of Mercy –'

'I'll believe you,' said Matt.

'Nell really is a very religious woman.' Tom said this so deliberatively that Matt burst out laughing. 'No, it isn't so funny as all that,' the other went on. 'Religiosity is becoming a job in this country, you might say. A plank. A threat and a menace. A power in the land, in fact, my boy! In the Island of Saints and Scholars! Yah – it's disgusting! It's a matter of municipal policy now wearing this little button and that little badge, holding a banner here and running to make a retreat there, with Father O'Hegarty warning you kindly about this, and Father O'Hartigan rapping you over the knuckles about that, and Father O'Hanigan running off to talk to the bishop about you! Town Council stuff! Pure jobbery. "But is he a good practising Catholic, Father O'Dea?" "And are you sure he leads a moral life, Sister Mary Joseph?" And if you aren't sure, will you kindly make it your life work to find out! My God, it's terrible! We need an Ibsen here, Matt. Is that your line? Have you returned to save your people?'

'But if it's true that religion has become a job, where do you come in? You do pretty well, I gather – and yet if you're allowed to talk like this, there must be some tolerance left!'

'Yes, there's some. We're a brainy and cynical race, you know, however they shove us around. We reserve our true opinions quite surprisingly. But we're not public-spirited. We'll be passively tolerant as long as we can, until Fr. O'Hanigan scares the daylights out of us with some hint that he's observing our neutrality. We're afraid of the Church – we always have been, except in sudden spurts. Her dominance has never sat naturally and humanly on us, as on the Latins. Maybe our temperament would have done better if we'd gone with the Reformation!'

'It's a wonder the house doesn't fall on you for that!'

'We've created no art in Ireland, such as the other great Catholic peoples have. A certain amount of applied art in the golden age of the monasteries; a certain amount of Romanesque architecture, apparently; a certain amount of craftsmanship – *vide* the illuminators. But nothing pure, no fine art. No painters at all, by European standards. We have none yet. We don't understand painting, good, bad or indifferent. No sculptors, and none coming. Absolutely no composers of music. Although the Eternal Church, which we have served with so much passion, has been the mistress and inspirer of all these things elsewhere. It's damn queer!'

'There's the old excuse – poverty, persecution, oppression –'

'Never choked genius anywhere yet. There are no stifled geniuses, Matt. It's of the nature of the thing that if it lives it can't be held down. Talent, yes. No doubt the heel of the Saxon crushed plenty of talent – but no genius, my boy!'

'We have always inclined at least to produce good writers and good actors – and the native Irish literature has a character and strength which are downright impressive. The Bardic schools were good, Tom, and by no means naive.'

'Granted. We can, and do, produce literature – in proportion to our population we haven't done at all badly in some of its less pure, more applied branches. Because we are cerebral – I admit that – and we're moralists and observers and mockers. That's our line – when we're not afraid of it. Words we have some mastery with. The satirical bards had, by God! But you must admit, all the same, that the language we're now digging out of the grave has left the *world* nothing. Nothing like *The Canterbury Tales*, or *The Divine Comedy*, or *Don Quixote*. No, we've only produced one native giant so far – because you can't call Swift a native – we've only got Joyce to measure against the immortals up-to-date. And his great spring seems to have dried up on him now.'

'He's banned, too.'

'Oh, but naturally. Still, there's always hope for us when we're using words. Because we're moralists, I tell you. I am. I'm typical of the race. I can read, I can talk, I can argue – but there isn't a vestige of the artist in me. We're not artists. We have no artistic exactitude or detachment, no aesthetic purity, no understanding of the isolated, clear principle which informs all greatness in fine art. And for that I'm inclined to blame some clash between our racial makeup and the Eternal Church, which scatters artists, good or bad, like daisies everywhere else. She's got hold of some material here that she can't quite make the best of Matt! Perhaps we'd all have been more natural-like as jolly little Protestants!'

'God forbid. It's a disgusting theory. I wouldn't have missed my birth in the cradle of the Church – not for the chance of being Goethe himself!'

'Wouldn't you, then? The more fool you. He had a long, magnificent life, plenty of fun, and the most balanced mind in literary history.'

'He's welcome. I'd rather have been The Bard of Thomand.

... When Thady with a pack of cards
Was set in the midst of five blackguards ...

Tom chanted. 'I agree with you, maybe. Protestantism is a thought too tidy for us, Matt. I don't know where our trouble lies, to tell you the God's truth!'

'Is it such a trouble, though? Look at you. You're a malcontent and a talker, and a disrespecter of persons – but here you are, peaceful and prosperous in a town that you say needs an Ibsen to wither it. How do you account for that?'

'The passive tolerance of those few who are not too much afraid of their brains and who find me amusing; the shrewdness of the farmers, who know by experience that I'm as good a lawyer as my father was, which is saying a good deal, and that in the practice of my profession I abide by the law, which I happen to know; above all, my boy, the fact that I am believed to be well off, and my mother is known to be downright wealthy. She's mean all right, much meaner than even all her clergy-admirers guess, but she is afraid of the Church, and she thinks that eternal rest is something that you actually can't get for nothing. How much she's prepared to gamble on the purchase, her will will finally reveal – but meantime, I'm her son, and though certain clergy gentlemen don't like me – I can quote Aquinas to confound them, God help us, and they hate that like cocoa – still, I'm Mrs. Mahoney's only child, I'd have you know – a bad man to quarrel with. Besides, I pay my dues, and I support the Eternal Church, which I detach with exactitude from all this new parish ignorance and darkness. I know its tremendous history and all the black sins on its aged face – and I admire it as I admire no other phenomenon of human organisation. I never go to church or chapel, but I'm nothing if I'm not an upholder of the One, Holy, Catholic and Apostolical. And I bet you anything you like, Matt, that I'll die in the odour of sanctity, fortified by all the rites –'

'*Per istam santam unctionem ...*' said Matt.

'Yes – it's a magnificent way to say goodbye to life. I hope I'll be conscious when the moment comes.'

'But since you're supported by such an edifying faith, Tom, what is your objection to the natural piety of your cousin Nell?'

'Natural piety – that's a nice thing in a nice woman. If we'd more of it in this house, and less good works –'

'You're speaking with feeling, man!'

'My God, I always speak with feeling! But these Legions of Mary, and Catholic Actions and Knights of Saint Joseph! What are they at? The Church has been with us for two thousand years approx. – but now all of a sudden in the last ten years it's occurred to these gentry to invent it for us! Oh, I know it's customary to wave a tolerant hand and say they do good work in certain ways. Maybe they do. Maybe there are creatures so beaten and dispirited that they like to have a lot of smiling, immaculate ladies poking round in their private lives, and telling them to go here, and stay away from there and wipe off that lipstick. But the thing is wrong philosophically – this amateurish impudence is not a sane way to redeem the world! It causes an immediate discomfort in the brain – you know it does. The Church has had its eternal methods for the destitute, and for those who desire to be guided aright. They weren't broad enough or founded deeply enough in Christian Communism – but they could be expanded by an intelligent hierarchy. Expansion mightn't work, and their day may be done. But this other pious nonsense is no true palliative, I'll swear. And anyway, Nell should have more wit than to risk making a prim, interfering fool of herself!'

'But does she do that?'

'I think so. She's all for Dev, for the greatest good of the greatest number, and the end justifying the means. She despises individualism, she says, and all its cheap escapes. Cheap escapes, forsooth! She's for the law, for order and decency and obedience, and the great White Chief in Leinster House! I tell her 'tis in Russia she should be – that Stalin is waiting for her. That sets her mad. She's like the rest of the world, Matt – all she wants is to be locked up, and to have it in writing – from Dev, I suppose – that everyone else is locked up, too!'

'It's amazing! Even here!'

'Yes. It's the world disease – variations only arise from varying hereditary conditions. Here it expresses itself in an inflammation of that Jansenism that Maynooth has threatened at us for so long. Now it's ripe at last – and we're sick, like the rest of the world. But you can't argue with Nell. She knows all the answers. She's a historian, if you please, and she knew all your arguments long before you framed them. She drank in all knowledge at the feet of Professor John Marcus O'Sullivan – and took First Class Honours. You can't fluster Nell, who at least doesn't need whiskey to talk on!' He made a comic attempt to mimic her clear, light voice.

'But why do you mind so much?'

'Mind? Do I seem to?' Tom laughed and pitched his cigar into the fireplace. 'Divil a mind, my son.' His tone changed to good-humoured musing. 'Only I sometimes suspect that her whole attitude is a put-up job, a sort of unconscious mulish comeback at me. If my guess is right, I don't like the responsibility.'

'Why should it be a comeback at you?'

'Oh, God knows! But we annoy each other. We're antipathetic, and we're obstinate. And we both have what I can only call rather exaggerated temperaments.'

'That's true.'

'We force each other to be much more ourselves than we need be. It's a peevish kind of game – but I hope it won't turn Nell into an impossible person.'

'Or you.'

'Oh, the worst it could do to me is make a drunkard of me.'

There was silence. Tom selected another cigar, clipped and lighted it with great concentration and with an expression of amusement creeping round his mouth – an expression which Matt did not understand but found vaguely insincere.

Tom blew a long whiff of smoke.

'We were once engaged to be married, Nell and I,' he said lightly.

Matt was careful to register only a mild reaction of interest.

'Indeed? And why didn't you marry?'

'Oh, it's a long time ago – temperamentally unsuited.

First cousins anyway. Wouldn't have worked at all. Xanthippe and Socrates –'

'Well, if Xanthippe was one-half as beautiful, Socrates didn't have such a very bad time, my dear chap.'

'You think her beautiful?' Tom's voice was perfectly detached. 'Not many would agree with you. Una is much more admired.'

'Una's a sweet cabbage-rose – but this other has a complicated kind of beauty.'

'I suppose so. She *is* caviar to the general, certainly. In Mellick she is not particularly admired. Though she's had her share of honest-to-God suitors. There are a great many plucky men in the world.'

'Does she show signs of accepting one of them?'

'Oh, I don't know if there's anyone on the trail lately – but to my knowledge she hasn't had much use for the gentry that used to call around. It was amusing to watch sometimes. She has a deadly way of making a man feel that he hasn't quite got her attention. Brutally delicate trick.'

'Probably isn't a trick at all, but the plain truth.'

'I don't know. She's very defensive. But she ought to marry one of them. That'd put a stop to all her high hat nonsense before it's too late. Teaching is the very worst thing for Nell. What she needs is someone to shout her down, and knock hell out of her. Marriage, in fact.'

Matt wanted more information and felt about for the best approach to it.

'I wonder why *you* became engaged to her,' he mused on a lazy tone.

'Oh, when she came tripping down from college with her MA diploma under her arm, she was a very, very lovely wench, my boy. It was 1926 – I was 26 and she was 22. I was very susceptible as a young fellow, Matt – you may remember? And I suddenly realised that this kid, who'd been my sister, was a beautiful woman, and by God's mercy *not* my sister. I had a great opinion of myself – and I lost no time about courting her. So we became engaged and bought the ring. And mother and various people were against it – consanguinity and all the rest. But we didn't care. We wrote off to the Pope for his kind permission. And before it came we had an almighty, glorious row, and Nell flung the ring at me and flounced off abroad for herself.'

'Well – and then what?'

'Stayed abroad for two solid years – until Una, who was worrying about her, worked my mother into believing that she simply must have Nell's assistance and companionship for her old age – and tricked Nell into coming back. And here she is.'

'And what did you say to each other when she came back?'

'What would we say? Nothing at all, man. Welcome home, Nell. How are you, Tom? Since the day she threw the ring at me we haven't mentioned our fit of youthful amorousness, I'm glad to say.'

'Why did she take up teaching?'

'More of her nonsense, that. When she came back from abroad she became interested in perfecting her Irish – spent summers in the Gaeltacht. She speaks it fluently now – of course she has to for her work. She teaches world history in Irish, I'd have you know! Well, that brought her in touch with a lot of our native pedagogues, and she grew interested in education. She's a bossy character, you see. And about then her income began to shrink. They have some money, these two girls, but it's tied up in things that have dropped of late. However, there was no need for her to be anxious – she'll be well off when my mother dies – and meantime, I've always tried to make her see that any sane female would take a salary for all the time and energy mother exacts from her one way and another. But you might as well be talking to Nelson's Pillar. She decided to have a job – and her old *alma mater* was delighted to give her one.'

'I think she's right. Damn it, you might marry any minute, and then she'd hardly desire to stay on here –'

'That's true. But why doesn't she marry herself?'

'I should think she will.'

'She's thirty-three.'

'That's not so dreadful.' Louise would be thirty-three eight months from now. Matt swerved from that thought to the distraction in hand.

'What the hell was the row about?' he asked bluntly.

Tom took a drink of whiskey.

'As far as I remember,' he said slowly, and Matt reflected that such an introductory phrase must in these circumstances be a false flourish. 'As far as I remember, Matt, it was about another woman. Yes, indeed – it was. And it took place in this very room. It was a Sunday, about midday. She had just come in from Mass and was talking to me here. She was sitting on that desk, looking very gay, and I was feeling mighty pleased with myself. There were some letters on the desk that I hadn't opened – the Saturday afternoon post. I'd been out with her the day before, and she was teasing me about my slackness, so I said: "All right, boss – open them for me, and attend to them." It was all a joke, and on we went with it. She opened the damned letters, and the third one – well –'

'Well, what?'

'The third one was from a young woman whose name you might remember if I mentioned it, a decent little shopgirl with whom I had an affair for about six months when I was a law student, and whom I got into trouble, as they say. She'd had a kid, and I supported the two of them, and everything was fine. No bones broken. She was a friendly girl, and every now and then she wrote me a silly little chummy letter to thank me about money, and say how "Tommy" was, and send his love. Well, it was one of those letters Nell opened, by God! Friendly and jocose and making everything as plain as the nose on your face.'

There was a pause, but Matt said nothing.

'That's all. The row began then. That I hadn't told her! As if I ever would, the little fool! That I could be so callous! This wretched, good-hearted, deserted girl! This poor little fatherless child! That I should dare to marry anyone else! To let her, Nell Mahoney, *cheat* another woman! The insult, the crudeness, the meanness! Oh, my dear man, the Lyceum that girl talked! The utter non-reality! The clumsy idiocy!'

'She was very young. She was in love with you. It was her first shock.'

'No one should be so young as to set up as God Almighty! Well, anyway, if she flew into a rage, faith so did I! We made a magnificent row of it, by God! And she flung the ring in my face, and swept out.' He paused and smiled at Matt, who made no comment.

'I didn't see her again that day. The next morning my mother told me with cold pleasure that she heard my engagement was broken. Una and Will never said anything. Four days later Nell had left Mellick – on her way to Italy, no less, where his Holiness was then dealing with our hasty request for his blessed dispensation to wed. *Voilà!* Old unhappy far-off things and battles long ago. We're none the worse, Nell and I. But the real joke is that a month after her departure I had another cheerful, jocose letter from the young lady in Dublin, announcing her marriage to a very decent fellow, a tobacconist. They have a large family now, and are very happy. I still occasionally get "Tommy's love" in the post.'

'Does Nell know that sequel?'

'I suppose not. I never told it to her. Have I bored you?'

'Not at all.'

'It's a ludicrously old-fashioned story – if it weren't a comedy of character it would have no value at all. But as a story of Nell, and me, I think it's illustrative.'

Matt smiled.

'You handle it like a master,' he said.

Tom looked at him with veiled sharpness, but made no answer.

Matt pondered the telling of the story. The slow, opening pace of one who gropes backward looking for something long mislaid; the quickening and lightening as the details come, the cobwebs fall; the outspoken tone of the conclusion, conveying so beautifully that now, having really exercised memory, the narrator sees the whole shape of the dead episode at last, and is willing to make it as clear as possible. Curious – because there was a kind of light, almost a patina, on these groped-for details when produced. 'It was a Sunday, about midday.' 'She was sitting on that desk.' 'She was looking very gay.' 'All right, boss – you open them.' These sentences did not seem like lumber. They had a sheen as of things cared for.

This lawyer had courtroom practice in the art of making every narrative produce a specific effect, and obviously the effect aimed at here, true or false, was that this of Nell and him was an old, dead story, long dried of emotion; a curious episode with which to illustrate character, and having no relevance amid present facts. The effect had undoubtedly been produced, and might well represent the actual truth of things – very likely did. There was no sentimentality or significant reservation to be noted anywhere in the phrasing, and such facial expressions as might have suggested caution or play-acting in the narrator would arise from an inadmissible shyness, uncertainty about the correctness of telling the story – simple embarrassment in fact. As for the rather touching lights of recollection – "she had just come in from Mass ...

she was looking very gay" – memory is random and irresponsible in every heart, Matt conceded. Some of our most vividly retained impressions seem to bear no significant relation to existent feeling.

Certainly the story threw a high light on the beautiful, bored woman upstairs – gave a picture of her young and gay and on the current of feeling. Crazily young and tiresome it revealed her, and with irrational capacities for pride and pain. Had she more or less forgotten it all? Unlikely. But Matt could not imagine her telling the story, to anyone, ever.

'Considering all things,' he said now, 'you go too near the knuckle in her presence. Why can't you let her alone? She's Puritanical, and has a perfect right to be that way if she likes. These cracks about Wordsworth's illegitimate child and so on – upon my soul, Tom, they're in bad taste when one knows your story.'

'Of course they're in bad taste. That's my point. Nell and I exaggerate each other. If she has a right to be Puritanical, all right – I have a right to be coarse. And coarse I'll be when I feel inclined. Besides – to tell you the truth I go on like that, I think, in a desperate effort to educate the foolish creature, to make her get the true, strong taste of life! A lost cause. But I'm a philanthropist, Matt, and I like to see human beings mature naturally. I like to see happiness. I like to contemplate spectacles like Una – decent human nature enjoying itself decently.'

'You don't surely think that the way to get Nell to mature into decent happiness is to madden her with what she regards as indecencies?'

'Oh, I don't madden her. She's not an innocent, you know. She's only too damn well read and aware. It's an intellectual theory she has of behaviour – that we should all behave alike, and only say what everyone wants to hear, that there are no privileges for anyone, that social duty demands certain taboos of speech and action, and that is that! I don't madden her at all nowadays. She just despises my anti-social individualism and my insistence on what she calls privilege. She despises it in you too, my boy. She has read your books, and says they are anti-social, myth-creating and unnecessary.'

'Well, I'm damned!'

'That's what Nell thinks too – though she's too highbrow to put it quite so simply.'

Silence fell again. A clock struck the quarter-past eleven. Matt felt uneasy now, and wished he were alone. Anti-social, myth-creating and unnecessary. Yes, indeed – and the gods be thanked. So might his work continue to be while the world remained the smug, dead colony of slaves he found it. Myth-creating. But his myth had vanished. Had beaten him off. Had grown common, cruel, practical, afraid. He was alone now and would always be alone – without his Muse. Without passion or hope, or any tangible sign any more that a dreamer is on the right tack. Unnecessary; of course – to everyone but himself, and in relation to those imbecile but irrepressible gambles for true fame which every artist unashamedly makes, and out of the millions of which the few immortals do in fact arise. But he was dead and tired – his gambling days were over. He had no idea on earth now of what to do or where to turn. Myth-creating. He had been debarred from that.

'I must go home,' he said.

Tom telephoned for the car.

'We must have later nights than this,' he said, 'when you begin to cheer up. You're dispirited, my boy. My God, at your age you ought to be ashamed of yourself! Have you no philosophy?'

'For two years I didn't need one.'

'That was a lucky run. Praise God.'

They walked out on to the steps. The wide Georgian street looked noble, beautifully lighted by cold arc lamps.

'Shannon scheme?'

'Yes. Good, isn't it?'

'Fine. A very credible-looking town. Up, Dev!'

'He's up all right. Good night to you. I'll be ringing you up for another meeting.'

'Thank you. Good night, Tom.'

He was driven home swiftly, through the quiet town and along the smooth Dublin road. The night was sweet and calm, the sky was starry. Peace crushed his heart and he felt his own loneliness upon him as a drowning man must feel the weight of waves.

The Third Chapter

Life at Weir House was animatedly tranquil. Matt, adjusting himself to the haphazard, gracious rhythm of the days, discovered the principle that informed them and so the under-strength of peace below the crossing ripples. Love was the principle – Una's very curious kind of love. She loved her husband and, deriving from him, her children, with an unheeding, unaware strength of generosity such as Matt had never before observed in an adult. He had never before met in normal worldly life someone who quite precisely lived for others. Una did that – as naturally as she drank tea. He concluded, watching her, that here was a woman who actually never stared at her own face in the mirror and said 'Oh, God, I'm tired of this effort, I'm tired, I'm tired I' Or 'I'm so good to that man – Heaven, I'm much too good to everyone I' Or 'I wish, I wish – what do I wish?' If Una was tired, she said so to Will, not to her mirror, and she rested until she felt better. She was no one's martyr and had no idea that there was need for a martyr in the cause of domestic happiness. If the children plagued her too much, she shooed them off without pious pleadings. She lost her mild temper with them sometimes, and finding it again apologised as easily as if she were one of themselves. She respected their rights of liberty and secrecy without having to think of doing so. She was completely subservient to Will without once remembering that so she had vowed to be at the altar. She was occupied in one way or another for her household all day, but her blue eyes remained unflurried and it was clear that, were self-regarding in her nature, she would regard herself as a free creature, a self-directed and normally selfish woman. And Matt would have wagered a good deal that she was without a fantasy life, without a daydream. All of her was in the here-and-now; she was complete. Without thinking of such a thing for a second, without self-consciousness or piety or even a breath of wonder, she was fulfilled. Will and the children used her up, and in so doing vitalised her.

It was amazing. 'Have you ever seen it before, Matt? Will you ever see it again?' Well, he had seen happiness before – had known it – but assuredly not in these terms. He had never known a woman like Una. And admirable and lovely as was her life, he saw that it was not a flower of some great virtue but rather rose from the accident of perfect mating. Una's nature, being thus and thus, had found in her appointed life its complement. Married to Will it was impossible for her, because of some reason hidden in them both, to be anything but that which she now was. Married to some other or not married at all, she might quite easily have been a failure. Not tragic ever, Matt thought, nor evil either – but a weeper perhaps, a lazy-bones, a thrower-up of the sponge.

But he conceded that the happiness she created and flung about her like light was not purely of her bestowal. In a happy marriage two are actively happy, and Will, though he played the quieter, deeper and less vivid role, was clearly as happy as his wife. But differently-arriving at it by the processes of a different nature. Una, though an entirely virtuous woman, was happy almost without reference to virtue, and rather by an aptitude for happiness which, being lucky in its essential claim on life, was too gracious and adaptable to offend against that luck. But Will was happy, Matt thought, by the straightforward exercise of virtue. Will was a good and principled man, and the principles he understood and valued most were founded in family feeling, and protected by household gods. Will was neither intellectual nor highly imaginative, but he had always been, Matt remembered, susceptible to hurt and love, easily depressed and touchingly easily flattered. A little pompous about responsibilities and duties, something of a lawgiver, but fundamentally unsure of himself, and inclined to the compensations of daydream. He had not always walked the strait and narrow path. Matt remembered that there had been anxiety about his 'wildness' when he was in the army, and afterwards, after their father's death, to settle down to the difficulties he inherited with the paternal estate had visibly been a bitter struggle. The sense of piety to past and future alone had made it possible – and then marriage with Una had finally forced upward all that he had of courage and principle. So that now he was happy – but as one is happy through reward and consolation rather than as his wife was, by very nature.

'And it is her final blessing,' Matt reflected, 'that she knows, or rather feels, that difference in them. Never forces him to be as she is, never strains his mood. Some part of her probably knows quite well that although their blessedness is by now an absolute rock, it still could be chilled or shadowed. The wrong kind of joke from her, an unseeing look in her eyes at a salient moment, the merest hint of a hint of unwillingness to open her arms to him – and my brother Will would be almost comically unhappy. By God's mercy these accidents, everyday for the rest of us, do not threaten here. Her arms are always waiting for him. She loves him – and by chance quite perfectly.'

Yes, Tom was right. Here was something not to be seen again, and worth a man's observation.

Children were a novelty, too. The three eldest, Liam, Maire and Sean, went to school every day – the former to the Jesuit School of the Holy Name where his father and uncles had got their learning, the other two to a kindergarten kept by nuns. They were driven to Mellick each morning either by Will or Una.

Liam took school matters seriously. Matt, lying in bed with tea, cigarette and letters, listened with interest to the boy's departure frenzies on the doorstep below.

'Mother, I implore you to hurry! Will you never understand that I *have* to be in the classroom on the stroke of nine!'

'My pet – if you miss two minutes what can it matter at your age? Anyway, it's just as important to find Maire's catechism!'

'Oh, Maire's silly! Why can't she keep her things tidy! Come on, Mother!'

'Here I am! In you jump, my pets. I'll drive like the dickens, Liam.'

'Do, there's an angel. You see, I really know everything beautifully today, so if we start with a fuss about being late it's a pity.'

The doors slammed and the engine roared. Matt smiled. Poor little devils, off to school – with their hearts in their mouths, no doubt. The goodwill, the self-control of children is very pathetic, he thought. So eager to tackle the imposed and get through it with credit. He himself had found school quite bearable, and indeed in its last two years, though neither markedly gregarious nor anything of a hero among his fellows, he had enjoyed it. He had found pleasure in learning, and had shone in the classroom.

Vanity insisted on that. A conceited ass in his teens – no wonder he had not been a hero like Will and Joe. But no, hearing the nervous ring in Liam's voice, he recalled the never-allayed sensation of panic with which each school morning dawned. Always, no matter how sure you were that you 'knew everything beautifully today' you faced outward from home into that world of noise, crowd and competition with your heart in your mouth, and a great sense of the long day's unpredictableness. A severe enough exercise on a young nervous system. Poor Liam! Nevertheless he was well protected by the ease of life at home – and by the lovely trust with which he viewed the world.

On Friday afternoon – the week's learning disposed of – the children came home in deep content, though Liam held out hands that were bruised and swollen.

'I got six, Mother,' he said. 'Could you rub some stuff on them?'

'Darling! Of course. Come along to the bathroom.'

'Oh no – after dinner. I'm starving.'

'But you ought to wash, Liam.'

'I washed just now at school. Washing hurts them.'

'All right, my pet. Eat first. Bridie, would you bring me the stuff?'

Bridie, who was carrying Una Bán, set off for the house. The family – except Will, who, having fetched his children from school, had hurried off again to the farm – was assembled round a large stone table set in the north-west shadow of the house, under a great beech tree. Here the children ate most of their meals on warm days.

Matt smoked in a deckchair nearby, half-reading *The Times* of the day before, and submitting with a patience, now becoming almost native, to the untying, removal and eventual difficult replacement of his shoes which the dreamy Peadar liked to enact many times a day.

Sean looked with awe at his elder brother's hands.

'What did you get six for, Liam?'

'Oh, old Madden. I got them because he wouldn't listen to reason.'

Matt laughed. That sounded the truth about most canings.

'What did happen, pet?' asked Una. 'Maire, do begin your dinner – there's a good child.'

'I knew it would happen, Mother. Oh, stuffed tomatoes – lovely! I handed up my Latin in a brown copybook – I knew perfectly well Madden wants them all in blue copies – but Reilly's *hadn't* a blue one in stock on Wednesday – do you remember, Mother?'

'I do, indeed. It's quite idiotic, this nonsense about the colours of the copybooks!'

'Oh well, he has a fad for having them all look the same in the pile. He's welcome – only he said he had told me three times – I don't think that's true. Anyway, I tried to tell him about Reilly's not having any blue ones in the shop, and he wouldn't listen. Said he wanted no more excuses, that I was thoroughly heedless. Anyway, I went *on* explaining in spite of him, and he said I was insolent, and had me out for six.'

'I must say I wish they wouldn't cane you children,' said Una. 'I think it's atrocious. Don't you, Matt?'

'I do. But what will happen now – if Reilly's still haven't got the blue ones?'

'They said they'd have them tomorrow. I've a Latin exercise to do for Monday – so will you remember, on your life, Mother, when you're in town in the morning?'

'I will, darling. But nag at me in case – keep on nagging.'

'All right – only remember tomorrow that you asked me to nag! I didn't cry, you know, Uncle Matt. That's my third caning – in three terms. Once I got twelve! I nearly cried then, I must say. I think I did cry a bit. Some of the chaps yell. But of course some of them are caned every day. They don't seem to mind a bit.'

Matt looked across the table at the little slender, silky-haired boy, holding his knife and fork with obvious difficulty, and talking with good-natured tolerance of the brutality of adults. But Una was standing near her son with a hand on his shoulder. She looked at Matt as if reading his thoughts and spoke with a lightness that did not conceal deliberation.

'You know we all think in this house, Daddy and all of us, that it's a bad idea – people caning and hurting each other, for any reason whatever. And we wish they didn't do it in boys' schools. But the Jesuits evidently think we're wrong, and Liam was rather scared about it at first. But Daddy told him to take it calmly and cross his bridges as he met them – and when he actually was out for punishment he found it wasn't so bad after all. Didn't you, pet?'

'Oh, actually opening out your hand is horrid – but you can bear it all right.'

Matt looked away from the little bony, unhappy hands. He wondered if in Una's place he would be as wise as she, and keep the unavoidable so steadily in normal focus.

'Sean darling – do try to eat a little more.'

Sean, who was not yet seven, looked tired. School was a great effort for him, and there was difficulty about getting him to eat when he reached home. Bridie, who had returned with Una Bán and the pot of ointment, strapped the baby in her chair, and sat beside Sean to coax him on with his vegetables. Matt, familiar now with the children's temperaments, followed the routine with interest.

'Surely it's a bad time of day to expect them to eat?' he asked Una.

'It is. Four o'clock – crazy. Day school arrangements are very bad here. They don't get a long enough interval to come home at midday. They take a kind of snack lunch with them, poor kids – and they have to eat dinner when they're dead tired in mid-afternoon. They ought to have school from nine to two, or eight to one, and then no more for the day.'

'Hear! Hear!' said Liam. 'You should be in the Dáil, Mother.'

'Aunt Nell would be better there than me. What's up with Aunt Nell this week, I wonder? She hasn't called on us since the picnic.'

'I wish she'd come,' said Maire.

'I telephoned on Wednesday – and she just said she was lazy, if you please, but that she might condescend to call today.'

'Oh, good. Won't she be shocked at my hands, Mother?' said Liam.

'At your being such an insolent boy, do you mean?' Matt asked, but got no answer, because a car came round the curve of the drive.

'Speak of an angel!' Liam shouted, and there was a general din of welcome.

Nell came over the grass. She was hatless and wore a very pale blue cotton dress. Matt, standing up to greet her, realised with irritation that he had no shoes on.

She bent over the table and kissed the top of Maire's head, stroked Liam's hair.

'Hello everyone. No, no – finish your pudding.'

The children were all wriggling out of their chairs.

'Yes – you're all under oath to eat a roast apple,' said Una. 'You've come at the wrong moment, Nell.'

Nell smiled a greeting towards Matt, who looked ruefully from her to his socks.

'You've caught me with my back hair down,' he said.

She laughed at Peadar, who staggered about with the shoes.

'Peadar, you're an old silly,' she said amusedly.

Peadar beamed at her.

'Big shoes,' he said, and staggered on.

'These children look rather the worse for wear,' Matt said, 'but I must say that no one would dream that you'd been at school all day.' He was unable to resist the crude observation because it was so true. Her girlish look had surprised him.

'Oh, I knock off at one on Fridays. In any case, the teacher has the best of it.'

'I got six today, Aunt Nell,' said Liam.

She turned to him swiftly.

'Oh darling – no!' She looked at his wealed hands and her face grew miserable, Matt noticed. 'Oh Liam, I'm sorry. It's horrible. I wish they wouldn't do it.'

'I knew you'd look like that!' Liam laughed amusedly. 'Aunt Nell can't bear things like this,' he said reflectively to Matt. 'She's not a bit tough. I don't know what you'd have done if you were a boy, Aunt Nell!'

She laughed with shyness.

'Then I'd have been tough, like you!' But she looked again with diffident compassion at his hands. 'What are you going to do to make them better?'

'We'll rub some stuff in,' said Una. 'They'll be all right tomorrow. More cream on your apple, Maire?'

She is not as wise as Una, Matt reflected – because she is not happy, or fully experienced like her sister. But she never will be happy in Una's sense, never wise as Una is. She is exceptionally vulnerable, and estimates human vulnerability by her own. That is what makes her sarcastic in certain moods. The defence of fear. Cruelty of panic. It is that too which makes her happier and sweeter with children than with grownups. She is emotionally terrified of adults, he mused, though intellectually more than a match for most of them. With these children she betrays what she should have been to all the world, what she probably was before she was unnerved. 'When she came tripping down from Dublin ... she was a very, very lovely wench.' Clearly – 'She was looking very gay ...' Could Tom conceivably be held to blame for a condition of unfruitful formidableness which now both alarmed and saddened in this woman? Could one wound taken in girlhood be believed to have altered the whole quality, and destiny, of a spirit which must always have been detached and capable of scepticism? Matt, philanderer all his life until he met Louise, with many shadowy places in his conscience which for the most part he preferred to leave in shadow, and moreover supporter through thick and thin of his own sex, shrank with impatience from the sentimentality of blaming Tom for a spiritual condition in this girl which, if vaguely troubling to the observer, was probably satisfactory enough to herself, and which, if irritating, was at least more interesting than many other possible forms of virginity. Besides, the thing was ancient history; she was a very beautiful woman, travelled, independent, and used to male admiration. It was improbably that the story had made any deeper mark on her than upon Tom.

Matt paused there, wondering a little about Tom. Then laughed to himself. This was real novelist's stuff, this poking at an episode which life had long since buried, cheerfully and without embarrassment. Character is fate, and if therefore there was any clue to Nell's in her one-time love for Tom, it was probably no more than the natural endorsement which her personality gave to that adage when she flew into her silly, girlish temper. No doubt a real knowledge of her life would reveal other situations just as formative. No sense in blaming Tom for an innate cowardice of hers, a fear of possible frost which kept the flower sheathed against the sun.

The next time Peadar came near, Matt captured his shoes and put them on decisively.

'No more of that game,' he said.

'Shoes,' Peadar answered dreamily and strolled away.

'Mother Mary Michael said I'm the politest girl in the class,' said Maire.

'Oh darling, I am glad,' said Una. 'Won't it be nice if you grow up like that?'

'The politest girl in the world?' said Nell, who had picked up *The Times* and was skimming it.

'Good God, Maire, don't be that,' said Matt. He found Maire the dullest member of the family.

'If the roast apples are really eaten,' said Nell, 'there are peppermint creams in the car.'

'Chocolate ones, Aunt Nell?'

While Liam and Sean pondered this pleasure and smiled at the donor, Maire made her way to the prize.

'I think Nell is terrified that any of my children may grow up to have as good a figure as she has! What do you think, Matt?'

He didn't like to say that it was clear Maire would not, so he smiled prophetically at the lovely Una Bán, who smiled at him from her wheeled chair.

Nell smiled at her, too.

'Una Bán will have a good figure – you'll be a beauty, won't you, my pet?'

'She is a beauty,' said Matt. 'Renoir should be alive to paint her.'

Nell threw him a quick glance of agreement.

'Do you do *The Times* crossword?' she asked him presently. 'Tom says it takes him exactly two minutes every night in bed.'

'He's a damn liar,' said Matt.

'Ask me some clues, Aunt Nell,' said Liam.

'Here's an easy one – "bounded in a nutshell and count myself a king of – space – Shakespeare," eight letters. Anyone got a pencil?'

Matt handed her one.

The table was cleared now. Bridie wheeled the Renoir beauty along the path; Una had disappeared into the house and the children disputed chocolate creams on the steps of Nell's car – except Liam, who sat on the stone table and listened to the clues.

'Bring me over a few, Sean,' he shouted. 'Go on, Aunt Nell. I'm timing you.'

Matt thought of London. He did not want to think accurately, for thus he would go straight to Louise – and pain. He thought quite enough of her when he was alone and she insisted – in merest justice to himself he might use the thin screen which the moving lives of others dropped before his eyes in the daytime. But now he thought of his own flat. He lived in Gray's Inn. His Georgian windows looked on a smooth circle of grass, two plane trees, and a statue of Lord Bacon. For six years these rooms had been home and anchorage; by degrees he had filled them with the books he wanted, and such furniture and personal possessions as he found agreeable to live with; by degrees he had made the old-fashioned top floor flat a place of comfort, and he took an increasing private pleasure from its peace, its unstrained and quiet beauty. It had always been blessed to get back there, always blessed to know, wherever he was, that it waited for him. It was neither a fashionable nor an expensive dwelling place, but it represented his material demand on life. Nor did he consider that demand excessively modest. His standard of living was not showy, but it was quite reasonably selfish and civilised. He had acquired with success no especial fads as gourmet or collector, but he lived fastidiously, and always, wherever he was, held with pleasure to the silence and the blended ambience of dreams and reflections that waited for him at home. The atmosphere he found there was that by which he lived most fully and most kindly. He was no family man, like Will. His fire was kept alight, not for wife or child, but for silence, or the talk of a friend or the kiss of a mistress – and at last, flaming to perfection, for the enchanted, flitting visits of a Muse, who had so completely loved the gentle refuge of these rooms, so generously blessed them with her love, so impregnated them with fragrance that now – she had bereft him of them. Now, where he had once been content and sure of himself, and afterwards so much more and less than that, utterly and recklessly enchanted – now there he could no longer stay.

But these were exactly the thoughts he had not intended. Not here in the afternoon sunlight, among children, and with quick eyes likely to fall at any second on his face. Merely he had begun by thinking that in running away from his own rather eclectic form of civilised life and in choosing to return for a breathing space to his father's house, he had probably half-thought – he could not remember now if this was true – that he was racing into an atmosphere of simplicity which he would find perhaps almost crude. Whereas – he smiled appreciatively – he was in a sense out of the frying pan into the fire. This situation of children and adults mixed together, this edifying home life, this atmosphere of active Catholicism, decorum, taboo and self-discipline, unlike his own life in all its circumstances, was alarmingly like it in that it was fastidious, self-conscious, selective and anything but naive.

Matt had lived many lives to which these adjectives could by no means have been applied. Starving, angry life of an obscure tutor, hopeless and without friend or drink, in Paris and Madrid; down-at-heel cafe-crawling life of a hack translator; orgiastic, crazy, short-spanned life of a young man who at one astounding blow sold three short stories to an American editor and received two hundred pounds. Thereafter, up today and down tomorrow, the literary life – the abandoned, senseless, exhibitionist life of London, Berlin and Paris in the late nineteen-twenties, through which, Heaven alone knew how, in cellars and lodging houses and borrowed studios, he had written those first novels which had brought him to maturity and South Square, Gray's Inn. The details, memories and remorses of these lives would not stand examination by the philosophic light of Mellick or Weir House. They were too crude and small to be considered by the ancient and snobbish sophistication of Catholic Ireland. A sophistication which had produced, but would by no means read, *Ulysses* – the most awful outcry ever raised about the powers of darkness. A sophistication which held debauchery as a vile and private matter, neither startling nor unlikely, but yielding nothing to the true purpose of life. A snobbery perilously over-nurtured – into cruelty and blindness – by the alarmist policy of the Church, but having, too, its indigent graces, as life at Weir House gave proof, and useful politically and racially. But untenable for better or worse by the artist, who can allow himself no snobberies, who can sacrifice his investigations to no policy, whose field is the hidden, the lonely and the individual, and for whom the five senses are eternally the paramount indications; for whom life's true purpose is, by his nature, the expression of life. Nothing more. A purpose far removed from those set out by philosophers, politicians and theologians, and seeming vain to them. But as constant as theirs. Most obstinately constant. Hard to plead for in any specific instance, childishly easy to dismiss and to insult, but eternal in its curious recurrence, and its deathless sense of its own unprovable importance. Always the same – without an axe to grind amid the shifting and changing from age to age of all the 'true purposes' of the men of action, thought or prayer.

However, this other attitude, not of simplicity, but of skirts drawn back from the mud, had point and distinction, Matt thought, considering Nell, the personification of it, as she bent with Liam over the crossword puzzle. God forbid indeed that any of the mud of his career should splash in this direction!

Curious, however, that his recent life – the six years which might be called his civilised period – being entirely at loggerheads philosophically with this that he found at home, the two should yet be quite justly describable by the same adjectives: fastidious, self-conscious, selective, and by no means naive. He wondered what this girl, for instance, would make of his life and that of his friends.

On the surface it would not alarm her. Wildness was *vieux jeu* now; exhibitionism and the orgiastic party were dead. Everyone was busy, either with his own work or with Communism, Fascism or the Oxford Group. Everyone went home early, because tomorrow was a very hard day. Everyone was straining to make money; practically everyone was married and had children. Manners were mostly good and discretion was *de rigueur.* Life was quite serious and adult.

But it was what this girl would, accurately enough, call pagan. And she would, of course, mean it opprobriously. No one boasted, protested, or made scenes any more, but everyone lived as he chose and said – except in politics – what he chose. Adultery and homosexuality were entirely respectable so long as their practitioners had the *savoir faire* to keep them so. Any joke whatever was respectable, so long as it was a good joke. Any word was permissible almost anywhere, by either sex. But tolerance and discretion were the passwords in regard to actual life. Go as you please and make no scenes.

No, Nell would not like it. All the discretion on earth would not fool her. She would smell rankness. And the free language of society would offend her beyond bearing.

What would she have thought, for instance, had she been taken to *The Country Wife,* and seen a play which was strong enough meat for the limited, debauched, theatre-going handful of the Restoration Court received with casual appreciation and immediate and blithe understanding by huge, packed, popular Old Vic audiences, men, women and near-children, husbands and wives, brothers and sisters? A sign of the times indeed – and one which would have strengthened Nell more than ever in her discipline, censorship and obedience.

Had you pleaded that there were excuses, that the *Zeitgeist* marched inexorably, that the creatures struggling in this present welter of cynicism and not-knowing were decent people, and troubled; parents often and therefore all the less willing to say, as the preceding decade had said, 'After us the deluge'; that they were, in fact, panic-stricken about that deluge, and therefore all over Europe were running to this and that ideology, only begging to be set in order, bullied, made to behave – she would very likely concede these points, but would say that their panaceas were materialistic and that a man can only be saved through the soul. To which one might reply – without hope of her believing it, for she was intolerant – that the mad world mostly knows that in its heart, and is aware of its spiritual death, however unable or unwilling to seek resurrection on, say, her ruthless and dictatorial terms. She would lose interest then – unable to be patient with the spiritual consciousness and anxiety of the incorrigible non-believer. For her undoubtedly men were either practical, practising believers, or materialists, what she called – no doubt thinking she insulted them – pagans. That a 'pagan' might hold the materialistic philosophy to be nothing, or at best only a contribution to politics and might live and die in meta-physical preoccupation was something she would probably not believe. That a man might be quite sure that life is informed by a mystery, and equally sure that that mystery has never been revealed and never will be revealed to human mind – that proud and final metaphysic of acceptance would meet blank scorn in her grey eyes. And she would think that there is only a good way of living or a bad way. You must either be for or against the Ten Commandments. That you could live a whole life, keeping out of jail and not becoming a pariah, without once remembering their existence – would she believe that? And turning her heel on contemporary society, how could she be persuaded that for some who account themselves as proud as she and creatures of the same maltreated God, the whole thing, the whole scheme is necessary – to be known, to be lived with and understood; that good and bad are not their testing terms, but true and false; that life as it comes is their life, without reference to Sunday sermons; and that sometimes in secret places of it that would be to her as pitch they find their own best evidences that man is a spirit?

He wondered amusedly why his thoughts attacked her with such solemn gusto on this pleasant, lazy afternoon. Was he pleading Tom's cause? The latter wouldn't thank him – he was used to conducting defences, but had evidently long ago decided against appeal in this court.

'Have you finished it? Your two minutes were up ages ago!'

'We've done a lot – haven't we, Liam? What's a "soothing job for an author" – eight letters?'

Una came and sat at the table with a work basket.

'Shall I help you darn?' Nell asked her.

'Indeed you won't and thank you kindly!' They both laughed. 'Do you remember, Liam, how a darn of Aunt Nell's nearly crippled you for life? Have you any socks you want mended, Matt? Or are you too grand to wear mended socks?'

'Much too grand, thank you, Una.'

'I suppose people really do despise darned things nowadays?'

'Definitely. A girl with a ladder is very much nicer than a girl with a darn.'

Liam was deeply interested.

'Really, Uncle Matt?'

Una was amused.

'What a wicked, lazy world you come from, Matt!'

'But that's not a moral issue, Una! Purely a question of taste.'

'I'm tired of this puzzle,' said Nell. 'Come on down to the river, Liam, and we'll see if the salmon are jumping.'

'Oh yes!' The boy sprang off the table. 'Hi, Sean! What about my peppermint creams?'

Nell and he strolled off together. Una eyed them gently as they went.

'That child is devoted to Nell,' she said. 'It's funny how children like her.'

'Funny?'

'Well, she's quite off-hand with them – and rather a severe temperament, don't you think?'

'I – I hardly know her, Una. But children don't usually like gushers, do they?'

'No. Certainly no one could call Nell a gusher. But she ought to have married and had children of her own.'

'Very likely she will.'

'Oh, I don't know. She's impossible to please. Once she was –' Una's voice trailed off and Matt, looking at her cautiously, saw that she was not, after all, going to tell him just now about the long-ago engagement to Tom. For intuitive reasons, he surmised, which she could not have defined, and did not feel entirely happy about. For he apprehended in his sister-in-law in this moment the birth of an innocent idea which she could not altogether dismiss or completely welcome. Would this Matt Costello, this unknown quantity, be by any chance a likely or a good, husband for her sister? Would such an idea ever enter his head, and if it did, how would Nell receive it?

It was a curious thing about that girl, Una reflected now, that when any clearly suitable man was paying court to her, anyone who, by Nell's own standards, had the right rules of living and the right point of view, she allowed the interested looker-on to entertain no hope at all that the affair would end in marriage, whereas now and then in relation to unsuitable people who visibly irritated and shocked her – Tom, say; or this immoral dark horse, Matt – one got a curious, indefinable feeling that Nell's reaction was complicated and its outcome unpredictable.

Una sighed, and re-threaded her needle. Intricate people saddened her somewhat at close range. Sometimes Nell made her feel very sad. She disliked the austere loneliness of her sister's life and its long, desiccated-seeming future. At the time of the affair with Tom, which had followed very close on her own marriage to Will, she had secretly disapproved of the engagement. First cousins, and obviously made to be at loggerheads! But as the years revealed Nell's serene indifference to this attractive man and that, as both remained unmarried and apparently something like friends, she had sometimes lately expressed to Will an uncertain hope that the two might yet patch up their ancient quarrel, whatever it was. And Will had smiled and kissed her and said that perhaps they would. And Una went on worrying vaguely. After Will and her children, Nell was the person on earth most dear to her. The reserved and formidable facade of her personality meant nothing to Una, who, delighted with her newborn sister when first lifted up to peep at her in her cradle, had ever since found her an amusing playmate, a simple and gentle companion and throughout life her true, dear friend. Una loved Nell very much, and desired for her such happiness as she herself had found. And just now, as she came out of the house towards the group under the beech tree, seeing how friendly they looked and that Matt's eyes were in fact reflective and kind as they rested on Nell's bent head, she had wondered – with surprise and some faint uneasiness – if perhaps an unforeseen solution might not lie ahead.

It would be a very good thing for him in any case, Una thought amusedly. It would probably mean that he would settle down over here, become a respectable Irishman again and start writing books for which his relations need not blush. But would he dream of doing it? Was he in love with some fast, hard creature in England? And, in fact, did Nell attract him at all? He must surely see that her figure and her white skin were unbeatable the world over and that her eyes, so grey and clear, were lovely. But her long, queer face – Una wondered. Nell was not the local idea of female beauty, and Una herself did not really think her pretty, but she had a very noble, aristocratic, greyhound look, and certainly a good many men of the world had been attracted to her. She was probably for sophisticated tastes. Well, Matt might behave as demurely as a parish priest on this visit, but there was no use in pretending that he wasn't sophisticated. You never could tell. But would it work with Nell? And if it did, would such a marriage be a good or happy thing?

Una sighed again, and then smiled. After all, he was very nice and gentle, and he *was* Will's brother. He must have it in him to be a good husband.

Matt watched her face affectionately as she struggled with her difficult matchmaking.

'What's worrying you, Una?'

'Do I look worried? Darning pulls one's face about horribly. I wish I'd remembered to get some more fawn-coloured wool. Will you remind me tomorrow?'

'I almost certainly won't.'

'Ah, here's tea – thank God! That's another thing darning does – makes you thirsty.'

'Altogether, it's a rotten hobby.'

'Will you shout at Nell to come to tea?'

He did not feel he could quite do that, so he walked down towards the riverbank to summon her more politely. She and Liam were coming in his direction along the path, with the sun in their eyes and on their hair. There was some physical resemblance between them, and Matt thought now that they looked like mother and son. Strange, he mused, that he had never really wanted children. A son like Liam, after all, must be a very valuable possession. Too valuable. Louise, he said, I am never again going to have a valuable possession. And day and place vanished for him behind her name, and the river was dumb. So that he halted, as if lost or out of breath. It's like a hidden disease, he said. Thoughts of her are as frightening as a menace of sudden death. Louise, let me go.

Liam shouted to him, and he waved. The salmon were in great activity, it seemed. They must all return to the river after tea.

The three climbed the bank lazily.

'If I bought a fishing rod, Liam, would you teach me how to use it?'

'Aunt Nell – I'd simply love to! Will you really?'

'I think so.'

'What's put it into your head?' Matt asked her.

'Oh, it's often been there. I like water and the things that go on round it. An excuse for being a Wordsworthian!' She smiled.

'Do you need an excuse? Are you afraid of Tom?'

That made her laugh. 'I don't think so. But mooning about rivers and places with nothing to do – one might become eccentric. After all, Wordsworth did.'

'Who's Wordsworth, Aunt Nell?'

'The one who wrote *We Are Seven,* darling.'

'Oh! Oh, him! My goodness!'

They rounded thc corner of the house, and found Tom with Una under the beech tree.

'Hello!' he called to Matt. 'I hope you're flattered to see me. It isn't often the Mountain takes his car to find Mahomet. And I find *you* here no less!' he said to Nell, as if surprised.

'It's a place you'll often find me in,' she answered.

'Did you drive yourself?'

'Yes, nice and steady. It was quite a treat.'

'It's a mercy he got here alive,' said Una. 'You really ought to feel flattered, Matt. I can't tell you when he last troubled to come near this place.'

'Hullo, Liam! I hear you got "tally-ho" today, for insolence. Quite right, too. Will you give me some tea now I'm here, Una?'

They settled round the stone table. Matt eyed Tom inquiringly; he found his manner somehow unconvincing, but the latter smiled with ready innocence.

'I took pity on you, my poor fellow, and that's the truth. Day after day moping round this idyllic kindergarten – and never a sign of you in the taverns of your native town. Is she making you give a hand with the sewing?' He waved at the work basket.

'No. I've been put in charge of Peadar. I find it quite an easy place.'

'Well, you have an evening off, don't you?'

'I believe so. Do I, Una?'

'Oh yes – sugar? There's no getting out of the evening off.'

'Good.' Tom looked as though he thought he had settled something, and Matt had a curious reaction of perversity.

Whatever this fellow was up to, he decided he was not to get away with it.

'If you've nothing better to do, perhaps you'll take part in my evening off,' he said innocently. 'I was going to suggest, Una, that we could all go to a movie. Would you come, Nell?'

'Thank you. I'd like to,' said Nell. Was there a faint light of amusement in her eyes?

'I'd adore it,' said Una. 'To tell you the truth, I'm just in the mood for a good film. The thing will be to get Will up to scratch.'

'Good, then that's settled. You'll come, Liam, won't you?'

Liam had been looking restrained and anxious. His eyes shone now as they appealed to his mother.

'Liam darling, I think not – there won't be anything suitable on, and you get to bed so late –'

Nell interposed.

'Una – do let him come. We'll find something suitable. Dash it, he got caned today!'

'Yes,' said Matt. 'Liam must come. You stop croaking, Una.'

'When I was young being caned was an occasion for censorship not for reward,' said Tom. 'Am I invited, Matt?'

'I began by inviting you – but I expect you loathe movies. Don't feel obliged to come, dear chap.'

'I'm a movie fan,' said Tom.

Nell laughed.

'Oh, Tom, since when?'

'Since I saw *Roman Scandals.* When was that?'

'Some time ago, I imagine?'

'It's the only film I remember. Is it on tonight?'

'Oh no, Uncle Tom,' said Liam, greatly amused.

'What is on, Aunt Nell? Shall I look for the *Sentinel?'*

'Do, darling,' said Una. 'It's probably in the study.'

'Tea in the garden, and taking the children to the movies! Upon my word,' said Tom, 'I think if de Valera saw you this minute, Matt, he'd tell them to serialise your works in *The Messenger of the Sacred Heart.* Please, Una, may I have some honey?'

Liam came back from the house with the *Sentinel.* 'There's *My Man Godfrey,* and there's Laurel and Hardy and *Modern Times –'*

'Ah, that sounds good.' Nell bent over the list with him.

'Is Liam going to the pictures, mother?' Sean asked gloomily.

'Yes, my pet. He's ten, you see. When you're ten, *you'll* go occasionally at night.'

'This place doesn't change much, does it, Matt?' said Tom. 'I remember distinguishing myself with a bow and arrow on this lawn once – at a party. I won the prize.'

Maire halted her doll's pram.

'What was the prize, Uncle Tom?'

'A penknife, I expect. I always won the prizes at parties, and they were always penknives. Do you think that arrow is still unbroke in an oak, Una?'

'Well, if you shot it, it won't have been moved – Will is very conservative.'

'I remember a party in this garden,' said Nell, 'and one of the Costello boys – was it Will, Una? – wouldn't come down out of the walnut tree, although he was being ordered to every five minutes.'

'I think it was me,' said Matt. 'I was always being ordered down out of that tree.'

'But during a party, Matt! How disgusting!' said Una.

'Yes, bad manners. I hated parties, and girls, in those days.'

'Indeed! *Nous avons changè tout cela,'* said Tom.

A telegraph boy came round the curve of the drive on a bicycle.

'Well, I never!' said Liam delightedly. 'Mother, what do you bet it's for Uncle Matt?'

'Nothing at all, darling; it's a dead cert. Liam can't get over having an uncle who gets so many telegrams.'

'Do you know, Uncle Tom, this is his fourth in six days?'

'I'll believe you.'

Matt went to meet the boy, took the bright green envelope and paid the delivery fee.

'There will be no reply,' he said, read the message as he returned to the table, and put it in his pocket.

'Another three shillings,' said Una amusedly. 'I hope all these sudden messages are worth the money. Matt.'

'Three shillings?' Tom asked.

'Yes. Sixpence a mile for delivery outside the city boundary. Up, Dev!'

'He could have them telephoned, you know, Uncle Tom, and then delivered afterwards like letters. But he won't!' Liam's eyes were wide.

'Naturally,' said Tom.

'I wish someone would send me a telegram,' said Sean.

'I will pet – next week,' said Nell.

'For Heaven's sake, don't! Another three shillings,' said Una. 'We're not all successful playwrights.'

'I suppose,' said Liam dreamily, 'that you have to be famous to get so many!'

'Or just a popular chap,' said Tom.

Matt leant back in his chair and pressing his arms across the breast of his coat heard the telegram crackle softly in his inside pocket. Family life. What on earth were they all saying? He smiled in desperate vagueness towards Una, and passed up his cup for some tea. He noticed with alarm as he did so that his hand was shaking. These senseless telegrams. He had come to dread the Free State's bright green envelope. Oh faraway, oh mad and irresponsible, to see you once again, but only once again! Oh savage, foolish, indeterminate, determined love!

'No sugar, thank you, Una.'

A man might be allowed to live or die. Who did she think she was to take this privilege of torture? He stared into the innocent heaven, and was conscious of great effort to keep still, to keep his hands unclenched and his features smooth. He read the telegram again across the empty sky. 'Pay no attention to these telegrams stop I know I should not send them but I must stop sleep well my darling and forget.' No name. Only her sweet irrationality for signature. 'Sleep well my darling and forget.' He smiled and was conscious of control returning. He withdrew his eyes from the sky, and found Tom's upon him.

'Bad news?' The tone was kind but alertly pointed.

'Bad enough,' Matt answered harshly. He turned to Nell. 'Are we going down to the river?' he asked her.

'Yes, I'd like to. Come on, Liam.'

'So would I,' said Tom with unexpected energy.

They descended to the river and sat on rocks by the roaring torrent whose glare hurt the eyes now in afternoon light. Liam skipped and shouted as the great fish hurled themselves at the leap. Matt held his left arm tight against the pocket in his breast, and set himself resolutely to watch for the heroic, upgoing curves of the great salmon.

THE FOURTH CHAPTER

'This is idiotic. But you know that. Common sense has never seemed important to you. Even your cold arguments in favour of marital virtue are not strong in it. I accepted them, however, and in return have only asked you to let me be. I implore you therefore to stop sending these telegrams. They are flippant and stupid ...'

He laid down his pen and stood up. He walked the length of the room and back to the writing table where four telegraph forms lay spread under the lamplight. He picked them up.

'Goodbye, goodbye, goodbye.' That was the first. Theatrical from anyone else, but from her who was all made of innocent theatre, a natural cry. The second was longer. 'Matt I think I'm dying stop I loathe the lovely play stop when did you say the worst would be over?' He smiled at that, would smile at it in hell, he thought with gratitude. It was her very voice, her ringing girlishness. 'When did you say?' – he could see her face lifted in sweet attention, blue eyes comically certain that Matt's wise answer would be gospel truth. Ah, what was this torturing friendliness between them that no despair could injure?

God, to hate her as her cowardice deserved, to despise her as her miraculous grace of spirit made impossible!

The third telegram was flatly inexcusable. A line from Donne, springing from their most illumined hours. 'For God's sake hold your tongue and let me love,' the telegram said. She dared to send him that joke now? He laid it down, made breathless once again by her impertinence and cruelty.

He stared at the bright moon. Somewhere in the quiet house a clock struck one.

He walked to the window and leant against the sash, looking down at the cold, silver river. He was glad of the flowery breeze on his face.

He was willing to believe that Louise's physical beauty could be matched and even that her open, visible qualities of grace and good will, too luminous to be described as charm, were possibly not unique. All that she was to her audiences, to her friends and servants and in the usual traffic of life might conceivably be found elsewhere beneath the visiting moon. But as a lover – there was no one else. After her the mould was broken. Alone with him and the night she was always, without fail, herself immeasurably perfected. He had never been done with the wild surprise of that. She who in her greatest moments on the stage could seem to be all made of light and benediction had still a pocketful of private suns for him. Safe in his arms her piercing friendliness – it was the word he never could escape from in his thoughts of her – took on the air of genius. As a lover, variable and moody as the sky, she could do no wrong. She was infallible. She knew him and herself by inspiration, and therefore had to take no heed, it seemed, of how things were with them superficially. Discouragement, worry, headache, jealousy, lassitude – all these were welcome and she was not afraid of them within the circle that she drew about their love, for all these things were her and him, and so be it they were alone and with time to love she felt no danger. She seemed to think that their passion's virtue drew the sting from human weaknesses. And she was right. Together they could not go wrong. Apart, or among other people, they could drive each other mad, and work up agonies of loathing and confusion, write savage letters, stare at each other out of eyes like stones – but alone again and face to face in his rooms, even if quarrelling still, even if weeping, even if shaken with rage and terror, the air was changed. Love, brilliant, variable and true as neither had ever dreamt that it could be, had them in charge, and they knew that, quarrel all night if they liked, they were fantastically, deliriously safe.

When he marvelled at this perfection that she brought to love, when he tried to thank her, tried to explain his perpetual bewilderment and rapture, she always said the same thing – 'But it is you, Matt; it's not me. If I make you happy, it's only because it's you; because we're perfectly right. I've never been this sort of success before, I promise you.' 'And neither have I, by heaven! Neither have I.' Sometimes she theorised contentedly, holding his heavy head against her breast. 'It's quite simple, you know, Matt. There's no mystery about us. We're happier than it's humanly possible to be because we *appreciate* each other. People don't, you know, as a rule. People in love, I mean. *Appreciate.* Oh, Matt, that means that you don't have to invent something out of the material presented – you just like it – my God, how you *like* it – there as it stands. I *like* every mortal thing about you, Matt – I've done so from the word "go". I *appreciate* you, my darling! See?'

She was like that – all generosity, clarity, good will and praise. Shrewd too – because appreciation was their strength. Sheer, cold appreciation of each other's general makeup of character, mind and body was the unique thing that could not fail between them, and that neither could ever deny. Each knew from beginning to end of their love story that the other was the human being they *liked* best on earth.

And now, with that fact still undenied and undeniable, now they were apart for ever by her silly command.

'For God's sake hold your tongue –' They had had fun with that line which he was fond of quoting at her; but she, who liked sometimes to play the bullying amorist, announced it one night as her motto. 'It's a great piece of advice and you've got to take it.'

The peace, the anchorage. Her face, young, white and weary, her curls floating damply back from the smooth brows, her eyes very dark with love. Silence all about them, far off the London murmur. In the heart a deep weight of multitudinous inspiration – her endless gift. On every nerve the drowsy sense of dream and time and safety.

He turned back from the window. Moths danced about the oil lamp on the writing table. There was no other light and the long-ceilinged room was profoundly shadowed. That, in accordance with Will's sentiment, he should sleep up here in boyhood's place and not in the traditional 'spare' room on the first floor, had probably meant considerable trouble for Una, and a re-distribution of the children. He would have preferred to be a *bona fide* visitor, but Will will would never see the artificiality of his own gentle notions. So here the returning brother must be lodged at night.

He poured whiskey into a glass. Will, who had been a drinker once and who remembered their father's weakness, seemed worried by his having whiskey in his room, but Matt could have no fraternal bullying over that. 'I'm a genius, my good fellow, and a night bird! Keep sober in your way, Will, and let me do the same in mine!' These married men. For them the human day was over at eleven pm. He smiled. Not quite over perhaps. Not every night. But about that hour it was certainly their habit and duty to call a truce to ideas and impulses, to shed vitality and become as little children, good and quiet. What an impossible undertaking, he mused – to guarantee to be sleepy at midnight every day of one's life!

Matt laughed and carrying his glass paced about the room. The night was his time – perhaps that was one reason why he had never married. Perhaps he had always known that he could never promise to synchronise with another fellow-creature's the putting out of his light, the closing of his eyes. Neither could Tom Mahoney, for instance. He was one of those who cannot be bothered with tomorrow's warning if tonight's idea seems a good one, tonight's emotion an imperious. But Tom, sensualist and intellectual, dismissed emotion as adolescent, very likely. And had he in fact taken a wife it was improbable that marriage would induce in him that notion of the average man that once his wife was in bed he also must, by some physico-psychical law, be there. Tom would never believe that he and any other could become one flesh. But if he married his cousin Nell she would insist on orthodoxy. No privilege, no eccentricities. Matt smiled. According to Tom, Nell would have the world run to barrack rules, by 'Lights Out' and 'Reveille.' If that was true it was as well that the two should not marry. Nor would they now, of course. Waste, it might be said. But probably the odd situation which their peculiar characters had evolved from their old emotion had more grace in it than either would have found by uneasily entering the common refuge. To marry for comfort or in fear of loneliness – both, being human, would have known the temptation, but each had that within which made it resistible, and two who were willing to stay solitary should, by all the rules, make a bad union.

He paused by the table, looked at the strewn telegrams and the letter he had begun. Louise! How she had failed and baffled him! How as it possible to reconcile her love with the dull and cowardly inflexibility of her ultimate decision? Or had her love been in fact nothing more than the most brilliant performance of her life, and was this obstinate, denying woman now emerging in her the natural, off-stage Louise who must, being human, relax, go slack, and put her feet up?

Obviously there were two Louises. But that was hardly news. There were at least two of everyone. She knew that as well as he did. They had been through a hundred panics arising from the ordinary conflicts and contradictions within their isolated personalities. Each had jibbed again and again under the strain imposed by the other's preconceptions. He and she were nothing if not exacting – and exhausting. But they had been through all that, and he, for his part, was prepared to face a lifetime of their wearing battle, in gratitude for its essential cause and effect. The absolute sweetness at the centre of their love seemed to him worth every kind of courage and mutually taken risk and blow. So she had felt too – or said. The great, swift-feeling actress, Louise. But now in the last three months this other thing, this weariness, this flight to her own commonplace, this savage and fickle determination to throw up her greatest part. To do it gracefully – oh yes – Louise Lafleur must be graceful. She must even contrive to kick a man to bits without looking horrible as she did it. Hence these tears, these glances back and pretty cries. Hence this nursing of pain in the stillness of relief and escape. It must not be thought for a second that she was callous – she must not have to suspect it of herself. Her heart was bleeding, but she must do as she must do. In fact, she must have her own way, and a little commonplace peace and quiet. Domestic dullness to tone her up, no scandalous, bothersome break in the *status quo*, and a final, obdurate goodbye to the too-stimulating, too-exacting passion of one whom, subtly to placate while deeply hurting, she described, and very humbly and cleverly dismissed, as a 'genius.' 'I'm not your size, Matt. I could never keep it up. I'm only a very ordinary female creature.' 'I haven't asked you to be my size. You inspire me – give me illusion and life. What does it matter what either of us really is? We'll never know. We only know – somewhat – our effect on each other. But I have only influenced the artificial side of you, the trained, professional side. For real life you want a very different thing than me. But why did you *act* so well, for so long and so often?' 'I didn't act. I love you, love you. But I promise you you'd hate me soon. I'm ignorant and ordinary. I'm *not* a match for you. Either I'd bore you to death when my looks begin to go, or I'd go mad trying not to. And there's Adam, and everything. You know it all. You know I'm weak and kind. Oh yes, I know you think I'm cruel too. I suppose I am. But you can take cruelty – you don't think much of kindness. I've never given you any – only love. Love is what you want – and I haven't the guts to undertake such a tall order for keeps. I always take the easy way.' 'That isn't true. It wasn't easy for you to become an actress, and to get to where you are.' 'Funnily enough, it was. It was a series of flukes that I had only to follow. I can *act* heroic and ruthless women, Matt –' 'Ruthless! I'm only asking you to get divorced and marry me!' 'You know I can't. You've talked with Adam yourself. He'll never divorce me.' 'He would if you insisted enough. The man is wax in your hands.' 'Exactly. That's the trouble.' 'Oh, my God! Divorce *him,* Louise!' 'I can't. There's no evidence. There never will be. Besides –' 'Besides, you don't want to!' 'No, perhaps I don't. For ordinary purposes our tame arrangement suits me.' '"Tame" is right. And within its tidiness there is no room for me. I've loved you now for nearly two years. For twenty-one months you've been my lover and have given me every reason to believe that was what you most wanted in life, what made you most happy. You know what it has been to me. But now in a flash, when the kind, condoning, self-centred, impotent husband –' 'He isn't *impotent,* Matt!' 'Oh no, not technically – but i*mpotent,* I say – returns at last from Hollywood, and refuses to have his domestic pattern broken up, his publicity spoilt, his fans disappointed, refuses to lose his façade as Louise Lafleur's magnificent and enviable husband – because he knows that he could never get another normally sexed woman of your fame to stay with him –' 'You aren't being fair! Adam and I have been through a great deal together. When I was unknown and miserable and desperate he was good to me! I'd never be where I am now if it weren't for him! No one on earth has ever been as kind to me as Adam!' 'Kind, kind! You English and your kindness! Have you no bones in you, no muscles? Life isn't kindness, Louise!' 'For me it mainly was when I married Adam. His kindness was life to me then, just when another man's unkindness had seemed death. He was already a celebrity, and I was no one. And he took me up, and made me feel tremendously important, and gave me everything he had.' 'Which wasn't so much! Why the hell wouldn't he? He was in love, the poor bastard!' 'It's no good, Matt. We can't get away with it.' 'We could, in a way, if you would.' 'You mean we could go on being lovers?' 'How quick you are!' 'Oh, don't talk that way, for God's sake!' 'How am I to talk then? Like an English gent? "Goodbye, little girl, and good luck. The best man has won. I shall never forget all you've been to me." And wring your hand until you wince, poor child. By God, I believe you'd quite enjoy a scene like that – vintage 1910.' 'Shut up, Matt.' 'I'll shut up when I like. You won't be my lover, now the big, useless blond is home again?' 'No – I can't.' 'Why can't you?' 'Because – laugh if you like – I can't live with two men simultaneously.' 'You can hardly be said to live with him.' 'I do live with him – even now. Although he knows the whole thing he wants me to. I'm the only woman he ever wants.' 'He's a magnificent wanter, is Adam!' 'Let him alone. We do live together now – more or less after the convention of husband and wife.'

'Honestly, Louise, I don't think most husbands and wives would agree with you there!' 'Well, we've no way of proving that. Anyhow, I honestly can't have a lover while Adam looks the other way.' 'Do you think it's easy for me to look the other way while he occasionally rouses himself to be a bit sloppy and domestic with you.' 'He has been my husband for eight years – there are claims and associations I could never explain!' 'In fact, you like the whole dull, easy, lazy, automatic business!' 'Perhaps I do – in that part of me that you could never find or even imagine, Matt. You swept me up on your marvellous, fantastic admiration to be something better than myself. You simply forced me to be your dream, your Muse and your illusion. And because I'm not entirely dumb, and because you have such strange vitality – I was your dream. I couldn't help it. You were irrestible, and made me believe that I was all the things you said I was. But I'm not, I'm not. I'm just a bloody good actress – and an ordinary, good-natured, quiet woman. And I cannot force this thing on Adam – even for you. I might, for a less exciting man – but not for you. Because afterwards with you I couldn't make the grade. I know I couldn't.' 'But I haven't asked you for eternal love, or a superhuman devotion. I'm only asking you take a chance, while we still love each other.' 'I would, you know I would – if I were alone.' 'Well, even if you're not alone, still take a chance.' 'I can't. I tell you I can't belong physically to two people.' '"Belong physically"? Whom are you reading, Louise? Where do you get these phrases? People don't "belong", physically or any other way, my girl. Anyhow *I* don't. Love is an hour we give and take, a need we fulfil in each other, a mood, a release, a perception. It is a span of time, recurring. We do not *own* the instrument of that – we use and bless and love it.' 'Ah, all these clever arguments!' 'They're more likely to be right than stupid ones.' 'How sure you are!' 'My God – not sure at all. Only frantic, Louise. Who is this man, this rotten actor Adam Wolfe, whose pompous, empty notion of himself must rule and destroy my life? A flapper's tin god, a Hollywood stunt, a magazine cover, a facade of glorious sex appeal. My God!' 'When you've lived with a man eight years, Matt, he isn't any of those silly things to you. Adam is my husband –' 'You've never loved him.' 'No. I didn't love him when I married him – I was in love with someone else. And after marriage there was a long time when I came near hating him. But in the end I find his plight very touching – and alarming. I feel responsible about him, Matt. He's not a facade with me. I've seen him crying and humiliated and miserable. I've seen him at his very worst, and at his most unhappy. I think I'm probably the only woman now around who knows the real Adam. Before me there were women – who wouldn't stand things, and left him. He has told me. You see how grotesque it is. He looks a natural ladies' man, doesn't he? Cut out for it, and he likes women. And they like him! Go to any of his films, any of his matinees. He has made an immense success on the suggestion of possessing immeasurably the quality he hasn't got at all – sexual energy. He just hasn't got it. There's nothing wrong with him, and he *isn't* impotent, Matt – just he is unimaginative and inept in feeling – and infrequent. He likes what is called 'petting' – real feeling seems out of his range. And of course he has always devoted so much of his life to the sacred business of preserving his physical beauty that – oh, I suppose a lot of virility has escaped into that.' 'And you are content to stay with such an ass, merely to help him feed his fans their illusion? You will sacrifice me to that?' 'I can't see him just as an ass. He is the man who was infinitely good to me when I wanted what he had to give. I took all he offered then and gave him precious little in return. Perhaps if I had been kinder, wiser in those first days, not so shocked and impatient, he'd be different and happier now. Anyway I climbed on his back to fame – however else he failed me. And he slaved for my success, and has never,

never grudged it to me. He knows that he's a limited and rather stupid actor, and that I am not – but he's never jealous. He's absolutely loyal, and gives his whole attention, at any time, to any business or professional problem of mine. And you see, this pompousness about his public, his gallery-girls and so on, these silly lies about him and me that he has built up for the Press, this "marvellous love" stuff – all that is his compensation for a lot of things that are wrong with his real life. It's impossible to grudge it to him, or take away. He did me some almighty good turns in his time, Matt. I simply can't hit him where he'd feel it now.' 'You've done that. All the gossip and scandal about us all these eighteen months he's been in Hollywood –' 'I know. And he's felt it frightfully!' 'My God, only the scandal? Is that the sort of thing he *feels*, poor devil?' 'Don't be mean. No one likes their name in the mud. But Adam feels that it can all be put right now, if we are careful! I think he foresees an immense wave of popularity for himself in the role of returning, forgiving, re-conquering hero!' 'Oh, Louise, Louise – the vileness!' 'No use grudging it to him. Success, and private failure, have made him absurd – even vile, if you like – externally. But to me he's just Adam, my wretched husband, who depends on me to shore up his whole scheme of things. You know that, Matt. I've always told you that I couldn't leave him, and that when he came back –' 'Ah, but you used to say too that you'd have to leave him, that you'd simply have to stay with me forever. Do you remember, Louise?' 'Yes. I remember. I often think that still. Oh, Matt, oh, Matt, my darling!'

Adam then would not divorce her, nor she him. And she could not have two lovers. No, not for any reason. Not because she would not but because she could not. She was brought up a Huguenot and the old rigidity lived somewhere in her still. 'And I was brought up a Catholic, Louise – and that obscure, unimportant Church imprints a few ideals too, you know! It wouldn't be exactly instinctive or traditional for me to share you with your husband!' Probably not, she conceded. But he, Matt, was more sophisticated than she, and far more disciplined. He would be able to keep his nerves and imagination steady in a situation which would only drive her mad. She couldn't do it, that was all. If she shared bed and board with Adam, then – 'Was there any reason why she must share bed? There did not seem to be much urgency in Adam – but did the fans require photographs now and then from the nuptial couch?' 'Oh stop it, Matt.' Adam could not be kept happy or working or healthy at all without the minimum of casual uxoriousness which was his habit – and if the whole wretched idea was to conserve Adam's happiness – 'or some sneaking, wretched backstairs happiness of your own, Louise, that I have never dreamt about or apprehended! People do, on the average, the thing they most want to do, given alternatives. You – let my memories torment me as they please – you want Adam and your Knightsbridge peace and smugness more actually than you want my love, or to be my lover and inspire my work and work in it! Adam is also, of course, a richer man than I –' No, that was silly. 'I earn all the money I want, Matt, and I've never noticed that you are exactly impoverished. Besides, you and your plays would mean far more to my career now, and to my ambition than association with Adam possibly could. I have outstripped him. Divorce from him and marriage to you would do my fame no harm. And I have never played so well in all my life as in *The Heart of Stone.* I could go on being better and better for you. You know that.' 'Yes, I know that. The new play is ready now, Louise – but, oh my God, you'll not read it. Do you hear? And after it there is another already begun – and another waiting after that. But you won't play them, my girl. I promise you that. You'll stay with Adam, and enjoy your own surrender – your own funk and vanity –' 'Vanity?' 'Yes, vanity. You're so afraid you'd fail in love with me, so afraid I'd lose my illusion that you have decided to take no risks with your precious, ideal self, but make a pseudo-heroic gesture, and let me die of a beautifully, sensitively, tenderly broken heart. You feed your vanity in smug self-sacrifice. My heart won't break, and I'll write my plays – the plays I found in your arms, in your face – but there are other actresses to play them. There was always this restrained, suburban, neat, inflexible you that I never had the wit to see – and wouldn't have liked if I'd seen it –' 'There was always Adam's wife. I never pretended there wasn't – or that Adam mightn't beat us in the end.' 'Well, he has. I suppose you think you're "Candida" and are enjoying the sweet pang of making her fatuous choice? One of the silliest and most conceited decisions in literature!' 'Either way a woman chooses can be made to seem conceited – you force that on us.' 'For God's sake, Louise, don't generalise, because you can't!' 'Very well. Don't you see – how useless I'd be to you one day, Matt? Don't you see that you've always asked the impossible?' 'Yes – and I got it, from you. Louise – I implore you –'

Reliving a hundred wild conversations of farewell he strode up and down the shadowy room. His slippers made no noise on the carpet and although he was unaware whether he spoke aloud or not there was in fact no sound save from the unresting weir. But Matt had forgotten his surroundings. So far as he knew he was in South Square, pacing the long panelled room from desk to fireplace, pausing to glance at her, to shout at her, as she sat, very white, very still, her curls untidy on her brow, in the Louis Quinze chair she had always loved to sit in. So clearly was he there with her that when he poured himself another drink, he almost offered her one.

But the faraway clock striking two brought him to a halt and to reality. The lamp was smoking. He crossed to the writing table and lowered the flame. Passion and anger whirred down slowly in his heart to sickening deadness. She was not here. She was asleep three hundred miles away. Asleep with her arms most touchingly crossed, like a child's, above her breast. Asleep with her curls in disorder, and the sweet pulse beating softly, softly in her throat. How often he had seen that motionless sleep – that he would never see again. What was it he was trying to say to her just now? What quarrel had he been re-living? Oh, a hundred of them, a thousand, all the same. She knew all these wild insults, all his arguments and woes. Useless, useless. In any case, she was asleep. Had he really begun an idiotic letter? He picked it up and read it, smiling. My God, he thought, I might be twenty-one, the manly, righteous tone of me! God help you, my Louise, how I must bore you! Oh love, oh sweet – if you would tell me what to do!

He tore the notepaper in little pieces. Then one by one he tore up the four telegrams. He did this slowly, as if he were an old man or in pain. Then he picked up his glass and walked back to the window. The declining moon hung just above the walnut tree.

THE FIFTH CHAPTER

Matt and Liam strolled along King Street. They were having an afternoon on the spree. It was a Saturday at the end of June and the weather was beautiful. The town was lively, therefore, and the Georgian street, wide and long, was a pleasant place for a stroll. Liam skipped delightedly. He loved streets and shops and in general the hum of life. Matt remembered how he too had loved this street when he was young and realised with a pang that had something as irrelevant-seeming as relief in it that he still loved it. It was indeed a very creditable street, and none the worse for having been properly surfaced in recent years; and so far, excepting about three or four new frontages, its architecture remained bland, practical and gracious as the late eighteenth century had decreed. For Woolworths after all, Matt thought as Liam pulled him ecstatically through its crowded entrance, Woolworths red face is now almost as unexceptional as church bells or a cat on a hearthrug, and more effective perhaps than a touch of nature in making the whole world kin.

He followed his nephew from counter to counter and debated with him the advisability of purchasing this or that 'novelty.' Liam liked what he called 'novelties,' but he did not care to waste money, his own or anyone else's, and his embarrassed struggles between pleasure and anxiety over 'Uncle Matt's extravagance' were sweet to observe. He had a most true politeness, that kind which arises when an alarmingly sharp sensibility is allied with irrepressible natural charm. Indeed it seemed to Matt, who had grown to love the child very much, that Liam was exhaustively equipped with the more perilous graces, and he could only hope that life, so sweetly loved, might for once be sweet to a lover.

'And handkerchiefs, I think, Liam, don't you? Woolworths have the best in the world. I can never resist them.'

'Really, Uncle Matt?' The blue eyes went wide with amusement. They bought some spotted handkerchiefs, and some bearing coloured views of the *Queen Mary* and the *Normandie.* 'Sean will like those,' said Liam. They threw their parcels into the car which was parked nearby, and went on with their stroll. During his first week in Mellick Matt had hired a car for the duration of his stay, so as not to be an added burden on Una, busy chauffeur, and also in order to be free to escape when he must with his moods and meditations. Sometimes, as now, he took Liam jaunting about. He would have liked to take Sean and Peadar too occasionally, because he found them, though Liam might have disputed such use of his term, 'a novelty,' but that would have meant inviting Maire too, who bored him. Matt was never willing to suffer boredom. So he salved his conscience by being traditionally avuncular with presents and chocolates – a sop for which Maire forgave him much.

He had now been a month at Weir House. He was leading an idle and unsatisfactory life, yet could not force himself to look forward or make plans on the basis of his new loneliness. The play which he had been working at in

London when Louise launched her decision of giving him up lay untouched still in its folder and he would not turn its pages. Nor could he find energy or desire to write anything else. He had not communicated with Louise since leaving London and for a fortnight now she had sent no telegrams. Everything was over, therefore; the affair was closed. He was alone, and free to make what he could in solitude of middle age, loss and humiliation. He was a successful man who had had and used his fair share of the days of heat and arrogance. He must emerge from them and face the maturity of life. With money, freedom and an undertow of wasteful pain in the heart. Not so bad. There had been two crowning years of crazy and powerful illusion – a good curtain. When memory eased he would find a respectable way of advancing on old age. Here perhaps, after all, under the skies of home. Here amid immaculate beauties of hill and stream that, inducing dreams, did not depart, insult or weary. Here under the drug of memory and tradition. But suffering too all that these abstracts would exact of personality? Could he face all that – the nonsense and untruth, the surrender of ego and integrity to nurse an implacable theory of the common good? Could he live in de Valera's Ireland, where the artistic conscience is ignored – merely because, artist or not, he loved that Ireland, its lovely face, its trailing voice, its ribaldry and piety and dignified sense of the wide spaciousness of time? Could he live here because here was the antithesis of her, because here was a morality that scorned and banished hers and his, a pious, Christian island where noise and applause and passion and the cry 'Beginners, please!' would never thrill the quiet? Could he live here, turning over a new leaf, turning back to an old – and forget her? Forget the pagan Muse, the eternal Venus, the wild, great plays, the stirring, high abandon of ambition, the delight of unlawful love – and live like the decent son of his father, even the son of his Church, that he was born to be? Oh God, was that the price of getting over her? Had he to run as far away as that, back even to the rules and mysteries of childhood, to lose her echoing music? Or, what in God's name must he do to purchase middle age?

Liam and he were halted now by the window of a sports shop. It was a good shop. Matt remembered it. Its present display of racquets, golf balls, bicycles and flyhooks was impressive. Liam had no intention of entering this expensive shop, but he was interested in its show of salmon flies.

'Daddy gets his from Hardy's mostly, Uncle Matt – and really you know he needn't. Some of these are beautiful.'

Matt agreed that they looked very beautiful.

'Liam,' he said suddenly, 'do you think Aunt Nell would be offended if you and I bought her that salmon rod she wants?'

Liam gave a skip.

'Offended, Uncle Matt? How could anyone be offended by a present? The only thing is – they're dear, the good ones, and I've only got four shillings at present, and I've invited you to tea at the "Rosaleen", and I imagine that will take most of the four shillings –'

'I hope not. But what I meant was that I'd do the paying, and you'd do the choosing and so on – being an expert.'

'Oh, I'd love to. But ought she to have a salmon rod? First go off, do you think? Ladies can't ever be much good at salmon fishing really, and a good salmon might easily pull Aunt Nell out of the boat! She's very light, you know. I think she could really only catch trout, Uncle Matt.'

'Nonsense. The royal salmon or nothing. The salmon of knowledge, Liam. Aunt Nell's an Irish scholar and knows his noble place in Irish literature. Who in God's name wants to catch a trout?'

'Ok. We'll get her a salmon rod. But we'll have to be jolly careful with her in the beginning. Oh, come on in! Is it to be a surprise present, Uncle Matt?'

Matt was already regretting his absurd suggestion and as he followed Liam into the shop he cursed himself. God, how rude and ridiculous she would think him – buying her presents, of all clumsy, idiotic gestures! What on earth had made him say so foolish a thing to the child, and how in heaven's name could he get out of it now? By no immediate means, it seemed. Liam was embarked on the business of selection and was in grave consultation with a shopman. The rod must be bought anyhow, and perhaps he could think of some wily device to get out of giving it to Nell. Persuade Liam to keep it himself? Pretend that dragging in Aunt Nell was only to make sure that he would choose a really good one? Ah, that was it. That was the way out of it. Calming down, Matt gave his attention to the purchase, only wishing that Liam would not warn the shopman quite so frequently that the rod was to be used by a lady, a very slim lady.

It was bought at last, with reel and line. Liam was in raptures. In a shop famous for its salmon rods this was the pick, it seemed. A dream, a beauty. Matt paid for it, and asked to have it sent to him at Weir House.

Liam jogged him. 'But, Uncle Matt – that's not the address it's for –'

'Yes, Liam,' said Matt almost irritably – 'I want it sent to Weir House.'

Liam hated to be parted from it.

'But can't we take it with us? We have the car.'

So it was packed up, and they emerged into King Street, Liam clutching the long, beloved parcel. Outside the shop door they met Nell Mahoney face to face. Matt could only take a deep breath and hope for the best. But the delicious situation of intrigue and surprise was overwhelming for

Liam. Mysteries and goings-on about presents were wine to him.

'Well, my goodness, Aunt Nell! Of all the queer times to meet *you!*'

'Why queer, Liam?' She smiled inquiringly at his beaming, excited face and then glanced an amused question at Matt who was feeling absurdly nervous, and therefore combative also. Damn it, he thought, what great crime is it to buy her a paltry present? Why should she be so standoffish? She's my sister-in-law, and it seems I knew her in her pram! What the hell!

Still he could not face the idea of having his silly impulse betrayed to her.

'God knows what he means by "queer",' he brazened as the three walked on together. 'Come on, Liam, let's put your parcel in the car!'

'*My* parcel!' said Liam in ecstasy. '*My* parcel, *mar a eadh!*' (The English slang equivalent of this Gaelic exclamation is 'I don't think!')

Nell always played up to Liam's exactions and seeing that he wanted a reaction from her now for some reason, she produced one.

'Why, is it *not* your parcel?' she asked.

'Yes, it is,' said Matt. 'How are you, Nell, and where are you going? May we drive you?'

'It is not indeed my parcel, I may as well tell you,' said Liam. 'Oh, Aunt Nell, it's really funny meeting you at this minute! Are your ears red?'

Nell, seeing Matt's nervousness, began to get nervous too, though she could not imagine why.

'I hope not, Liam. Horrid sight, red ears. But you two seem busy; I'd better leave you.' She paused on a corner as if to turn up a side street.

'No, no, Aunt Nell – we're not busy anymore – that's over. Please have tea with us! I've invited Uncle Matt to tea at the "Rosaleen", and I'd love you to come too – that is, if you think four shillings will pay for the three of us!'

'Darling, thank you – but I mustn't crash in on your party like this –'

'It'll be all right about the bill,' said Matt, hoping that the tea party might be an effective red herring. 'I think we'll manage to pay, no matter how much you eat.'

He was standing by his car, and he took the parcel very firmly from Liam and flung it into the back seat, slamming the door on it with nervous violence.

'Do please have tea with us, Aunt Nell!'

Feeling the atmosphere to be easier now, Nell accepted Liam's invitation. She knew how he adored to give his friends tea at the 'Rosaleen.'

The three moved away in the direction of the café, but Liam looked back anxiously towards the car.

'Do you think that parcel will be all right there, Uncle Matt?'

'Perfectly all right. How comes it you're on foot, Nell?'

'Oh, I *can* walk. My car is being overhauled a bit today.'

'That's all very well, but it's a most important parcel, you know. Have you *any* idea what it could be, Aunt Nell?'

'Not the faintest.'

This answer delighted Liam, who skipped ahead of her backwards and beamed mysteriously.

'It's a salmon rod,' said Matt with sudden decision.

'Oh! For whom?' Nell was aware of nervousness again.

'Three guesses!' said Liam.

Nell thought she had better play.

'For Matt?'

'No.'

'For Sean?'

'No!'

'For Mother?'

'Oh no, Aunt Nell! My goodness, no!' Pause. 'It's for you, silly!'

Matt had played for this and took his cue quickly.

'Well no,' he said with a conspiratorial smile, one grownup to another, at Nell. 'I'm afraid I was guilty of using your name in a trick. I wanted him to choose himself a rod he'd really like and think perfect, so I pretended we were buying it for you. I was going to give it to him when we got home. Do you mind?'

Nell smiled, somewhat mystified. This speech was delivered with a faintly excessive naturalness, she thought.

Liam stood stock-still, blocking their path.

'But no!' he said. 'That – that really can't be true, Uncle Matt! You distinctly said, all of a sudden, "Shall we buy Aunt Nell that salmon rod she wants!" Didn't you?'

'Of course I did. That was when I caught you.'

'But – but really – I'd never have let you – honestly, for *me* it's absolute waste of money. Oh, Uncle Matt – you see I have a lovely rod – you *know* mine, the one Daddy gave me at Christmas. I *don't* want a rod, honestly! Oh, it's such a pity! I truly thought you were going to have a lovely surprise, Aunt Nell –' the child began to realise that he had done something awkward. He felt embarrassed and small. He bit his lip, but Nell could see the bright tears in his eyes. She was unable to bear the sight of this child in trouble. She leant forward and took his hand, making him walk on with her.

'But perhaps I am,' she said. 'After all, if it is your rod, you can give it to me if you like, can't you? Uncle Matt wouldn't mind I'm sure?' She looked towards Matt and he could catch no vestige of mockery in her eyes. She was intent on reassuring Liam.

'I'd love him to do exactly what he likes with it,' Matt answered gravely. 'It was stupid of me to forget that he has a rod.'

Nell's face reflected no amusement even now.

'Oh, might I give it to you, Aunt Nell? You see I chose it absolutely for you –'

'Will you give it to me, pet?'

'Of course. You'll simply love it! It's easily the best rod in Doherty's – you wait until you see it!'

'I'm in luck,' she said. 'Thank you most awfully, darling. Thank you both.' She smiled very innocently at Matt. They entered the 'Rosaleen' and found a table in the furthest corner – Liam's favourite table.

There were a good many people in the cafe. The radio purred a sentimental song. 'Radio Paris,' said Liam contentedly. He was quite happy again, and he ordered a great many kinds of teatime food, ignoring the protests of his guests. 'I'm sure it won't be more than four shillings,' he whispered reassuringly to Matt.

'But there's the tip, of course. Still, Alice knows me. I could call in on Monday, and tip her on my way home from school – I can explain to Daddy.'

'Better not have it on your mind so long, don't you think?' Matt whispered back, and tried to slip him a half-crown under the table.

'Oh no, thank you Uncle Matt – not unless I *have* to, really.'

Tea arrived.

'We've got a record of that song,' said Liam. 'French, isn't it?'

'Yes. *Parlez-moi d'amour,*' said Matt.

'What's it mean, Aunt Nell?'

'Surely you know what *parlez-moi* means?'

'"Speak to me"?'

'That's right. *"D'amour"* is really *de amour*. *d'* apostrophe, you know.'

'"*De*" is "of".'

'Right again. You're quite a linguist. "*Amour*" means "love".'

'Oh! "Speak to me of love".' He hummed it gaily. 'How would you say it in Irish, Aunt Nell?'

She laughed.

'It wouldn't go very neatly into Irish, I think.'

'Still, say it some way or other in Irish, and I'll see if I can fit it to the air.'

'*Labhair liom i thaobh an ghrádh,*' Matt volunteered.

'You haven't forgotten it all,' said Nell amusedly.

'It won't fit,' said Liam, trying the Irish words.

'Oh yes, it will,' said Matt.

'Elide it a bit. Cream, darling?'

'Yes, thank you, Aunt Nell. Oh, wasn't it funny, all that muddle about the fishing rod?' The child, completely restored to gaiety, beamed confidingly on the two grownups.

Matt burst out laughing and met Nell's eyes almost challengingly. But she did not seem to see any challenge, and smiled with a kind of slow graciousness. She knew that Liam wanted one last reassurance before he said a final goodbye to his bewilderment.

'Yes, "funny" if you like,' she said. 'But mighty lucky for me. When are you going to show me how to use my rod?'

'That's just what I'm wondering, Aunt Nell. I'll have to arrange it with Daddy. He's the best person to start you off, and I don't think he can go out tomorrow. Oh, do eat something besides an old chocolate biscuit!'

'And get dreadfully fat?'

'You'd really want to be a bit more solid for salmon fishing, Aunt Nell.'

'As solid as you?'

After tea, which, with the tip, only cost two and sixpence, they drove westward across the river and up the Gap of Storm. Liam sat in the back of the car among the parcels.

'It's disgraceful, all the things we've bought,' he said with uneasy pleasure. 'Mother will murder me – but Uncle Matt is impossible to manage in a shop, Aunt Nell. Really. He's given me a book – oh, where is it? Yes, here it is. It's called *The Italian Masters*. It's pictures from all the Italian galleries. Oh dear! Mother will say I'm a greedy old cadge!'

'No, darling – she won't.'

'Well, if she doesn't, she certainly could. Do you think I might open the parcel and look at my book, Uncle Matt?'

'I think so.'

Contented silence fell on the back of the car.

'I hope you don't hate being driven,' Matt said to Nell.

'No. I like it – unless Tom is the driver.'

'I haven't been out this way since I came home. I used to love these hills when I was a kid.'

'They haven't changed.'

Nell was faintly annoyed with herself for having agreed to come on this drive. After tea she should have gone her way in peace. Instead she had followed an impulse.

She was weary these days and somewhat out of favour with herself. Introspection, to which she was prone, was lately an oppression. She lighted a cigarette now and searched her mind for something external and immediate to think about. The first thing that floated up was the salmon rod and she laughed involuntarily.

'What is it?' said Matt.

'It's not really a joke – or you mightn't think so.'

'Try.'

'If you'll forgive me, no.'

He felt vaguely offended. Was her joke on him? She knew his thought, but saw no remedy.

The salmon rod. She understood the muddle. He had had a normal impulse – normal to Irishmen anyway – to buy for a near relative, well, a member of the family, something she had said she wanted. He had expressed this impulse to Liam of all people, without stopping to think. That had landed him in the soup. If he had lived at home among his people there would have been no second thoughts. Tom and Will gave her this or that without a blush if they took the notion. Every time Tom went away he brought her back some extravagant nonsense and would have been amazed had there been any embarrassment about acceptance. But Matt was not used to being one of the family and had somewhat complicated his Mellick-bred impulses by becoming a man of the great world. And for some reason, though anxious to be friendly and easy, he was afraid of her. She could see that. So he had nearly died of anguish once committed to the fishing rod, lest she should ever dream he had thought of buying it for her. He had expected her to be offended – and Heaven knows, she thought, I'm so irrational that I might easily have been! Well, Liam had saved them both from an embarrassment.

She wondered how much longer he was going to stay at Weir House. His presence there was an inconvenience to her, for it was her favourite refuge – she was always content with Una and the children – and his being there bothered her and even limited her visits. Indeed, if she made, as she did, an effort to keep as nearly as possible to her habit of driving out with frequency to Weir House, she knew that she did so with the double-edged motive of irritating Tom and keeping him from suspicious comment on a change of routine. Irritation. Suspicion. About what? Tom had indeed a dog-in-the-manger temperament, but he had long ago given up bothering about her comings and goings, and he knew as well as she – they were neither of them fools – that this Matt Costello was courting nobody and that his emotions were in perpetual flight from Ireland. Here clearly was no suitor, and had there been, how much would Tom have cared?

But why drag in Tom? Nell looked sideways now at her companion. He wore no hat, and the lock of black hair falling over his eye made him look young in spite of the heavy jaw and weary mouth.

It was a long time since any particular man had troubled her thoughts, though marriage and children had as a rule seemed to her desirable – on terms. Her terms were high – if indefinite. She could often have had marriage and children but, since the break with Tom, had not been offered them where she could contentedly accept. Within the last year or two she had decided that she was getting old – and somewhat set in her ways. Old-maidish. She had decided, without enthusiasm, to be an old maid.

Now came this novelist, whose work for all its gravity and music she disliked, and whose temperament, as therein revealed, she even despised. Here he came home, with his broken heart absurdly pinned on his sleeve, and for some reason she was troubled, more conscious of him than she had thought she would ever again be of a man. It was an unsuitable and silly feeling, hardly a feeling indeed, rather awareness of some cold and still sleeping anxiety in the breast, but its threat was enough to irritate her. She marvelled that at thirty-three she could be even transitorily at the mercy of fortuitous appeal. Appeal – that was the novelettish, inaccurate word. She admitted now that that about covered it. For some reason Matt Costello appealed to her. She could hardly say she liked him, on the basis of an acquaintanceship so polite and carefully non-penetrative. He betrayed in himself no characteristic which created active dislike in her, as sometimes his books had done, but she realised that he was in no mood to seek positive liking anywhere just now, or to care whether it was given or withheld. And though his behaviour in Mellick was that of a sensitive and quick-witted man rather particularly on guard, she imagined that always, in greater or less degree, he was like that. She imagined that many people held him to be an agreeable man of outgoing temperament, and that some even thought him peculiarly sympathetic and quick in response – but that almost no one knew him. For that, she thought, is the penalty of being an emotionalist – you can only be yourself through emotion, and can only establish understanding and release authentic knowledge of yourself through the medium of feeling. And smiling a little she admitted that that limited the field of true association. His face, she thought, revealed even more than his books that he was one who must pursue life and control it through personal feeling. It was probably that only by deep and perhaps cruel or selfish knowledge of one or two fellow-creatures he had come to his present quite adequate novelist's equipment of general understanding. Emotion had brought him to observation, but emotion came first and would always be his sheet anchor, for better or worse. He worked from the particular to the general, but any sure, durable or broad-based sympathy between him and another would be unlikely to grow from the usual sources, similarity of outlook or tastes or pursuits, or from association or propinquity either – she suspected that he could be "associated" with a fellow-being for a whole lifetime without feeling anything about him – but would much more probably spring overnight into something like maturity from the mustard seed of one fluke phrase that took his ear, one movement of an eyebrow, one second of unexpected light on a face. From such things he could probably deduce and create with reckless rapidity, she thought. They were his food – and his poison too. But so he was. And because his searchlight by its nature flashed erratically and unpremeditatedly, there would be no telling when and where his intuition would rush out with acclaim, and complementary exaction. So, it seemed to her, he would be an impossible man for the really alert to like in the everyday sense of the word – though no doubt many vaguely believed that they knew and liked him well. The only way to know him would be to quicken to him in response to his own unpredictable quickening. Then, as open as a daisy while the mood held, he would give you all that there was of Matt Costello, and welcome. But you must move him first. That was the *sine qua non.*

Nell did not foresee therefore that she would ever be able to say that she liked him, since she could not like what she did not know, and she certainly did not visualise between him and her any such lighting up as she was sure was necessary to him in real friendship. But like him or not – he appealed to her. Against all her standards. She was attracted by his heavy-shouldered look and heavy, well-shaped head; by the obstinate and sulky set of his jaw and the gravity of his eyes in repose – Napoleonic, she thought amusedly, and Napoleonic too, very likely, the speed with which the brooding mask came to life at a flick. She even found attraction in his broad, soft hand as it lay beside her on the steering wheel.

All notations of the senses, she told herself, without embarrassment but with some self-mockery. You are having an odd sort of throwback to flapperdom, my poor girl, and we must assume from the line of your meditations that what this man is chiefly strong in is sex appeal.

Tom was right in asserting that Nell was 'not an innocent.' She was an unswerving, faithful Catholic, and a virgin. But had her temperament been quite other than it was, she would still undoubtedly have been the latter in the natural course of her tradition and because of the powerful control which the Church can exercise from without, as it were, on the most unlikely natures. But Nell did not merely accept the Church's rules – she understood them – and understood, more fully than Tom ever dreamt, that human nature for which they were framed. For she had a cool and ranging mind and accepted certain categorical imperatives as much because she was convinced of their general rightness as because all her blood was Catholic. Also she despised pleaders of 'privilege,' was inclined to admire dictators and to laugh at individualists. But although she would not surrender virginity without assuming in exchange the binding vows and obligations of marriage, this was as much a loyalty to her own intellectual workings as an emotional or religious inhibition. She did not think it necessary to seek one's own sensations at the cost of social confusion. One person's private love affairs might seem entirely unimportant, but any break in a principle was anti-social, and who was this one or that to claim 'privilege'? To her the family seemed the most natural social unit, and love-making that dodged the obligations of family was anti-social selfishness. Moreover, she could not admit, any more by her fastidious nerves than by her religious training, the pitiful exigencies or crude materialistic ethic of birth control – though baffled indeed, too, by the appalling problems and horrors of unchecked fecundity. She was, she knew, a good deal of a prig, but she was much besides, and knew that too. She was a woman who once, twelve years ago, had loved with innocent, foolish frenzy and had counted herself most perilously happy. By the measure of that innocent folly and happiness she had been most foolishly shocked and hurt – an innocent then indeed, as Tom had known. But that was long ago. Only it had taught her her own exacting power to love, and she had not forgotten what a storm of the heart could be. In the years since then, as she realised that it was not going to be easy for her to fall in love again, she did not hoodwink herself. She knew that in missing love she was missing the thing she needed most, something she understood and whose wild power she acknowledged. But a power which she would always fight unless it visited her on her own terms.

However, this strong emotionalist, this romantic writer was certainly offering nothing – no troublesome, brief love, no impertinent advances. This heart, beating so near her, was sealed and lonely. She was exasperated by the pain which that thought engendered.

'Pull up here,' she said, for want of something better to say. 'There's a good view from that bank.'

They crossed a field and climbed the grassy mound that she had indicated. The turf was dry and elastic. Liam's sandalled feet slid on it to his delight. The smooth green all about, pasturage only for sheep and goats, was broken by lichened boulders of grey granite and starred with wild orchids, wind flowers and Lilliputian pansies.

'I remember these,' said Matt, bending to pick the tiny flower. 'I once found gentian somewhere about here, I think?'

'I've seen it further west,' said Nell, 'nearer to the sea. I didn't know it was ever seen here.'

She had sat down on a ledge of rock under a withered hawthorn tree. She pulled off her shady hat and her fine hair was lifted off her brows by the gentle breeze. She was unquestionably very beautiful by captious, not by common, standards – Matt conceded now and, as perhaps twenty times before in the month, was irritated by a sense of formless, pointless battle within him over the concession. Why in Heaven's name should she not be beautiful?

But – summer becomes *her* too, he thought wearily. He had always felt that Louise wore June as her own especial garland and that she was the epitome of all its grace. The English summer of roses and scattered stars and the faint breath of meadowsweet. Here was another June – a little colder, not so flowery. Suited to this high place, for instance, and almost amusingly dramatised, or symbolised, by granite rocks the colour of her eyes, and by the slim withered hawthorn tree curved tragically against the sky behind her. Austere for June, and perhaps prematurely a little tired; but without doubt – he had pondered this before – wearing the distinction of her beauty the more emphatically in these brilliant days and under the searching light, and paradoxically with her suggestion of coolness only enhanced.

'I think I'll get a really good orchid root for Mother,' said Liam, and browsed over the field in search of the best available.

'There it is,' said Nell, 'there's your view. We all come out to see it when – when we want to be reassured.'

'About what?'

'Oh, about not living in Rome perhaps, or about life flying by while we haven't seen China or Mexico or Finland!'

'Have you lived in Rome?'

'Yes. I once spent about two years in Italy – most of the time in Rome. I – I don't think there can be anything more noble than Rome under the sun.' She grew nervous suddenly and snapped her cigarette case open. He lighted her cigarette and noticed as he did so that her eyelashes, dropped against her pale cheek, were tipped with gold. This subtle brightness was youthful – and touching, he thought. He turned away to the view he had desired to see.

Mellick lay at the heart of it, in the green, watered valley. A gravely poised city, old and quiet; the river swung beside it and outward south and west in brilliant loops and unfurlings towards the sea. The Vale of Honey spread east in summer richness to Tipperary's mountains, blue but even now snow touched upon the peaks. Westward, in the fore ground, the green and granite country, already expectant of the sea, shelved up in desolation.

'When I was a kid,' said Matt, 'we were always biking up here on school holidays and so on, and I remember that this view used to make me feel panic-stricken, of all things!'

'Well – it does seem terribly self-sufficient. I call imagine that it might damp ambition – and I expect you were ambitious!'

'I think I was – and I suppose I didn't take kindly, to all this bland and impressive indifference!'

'Do you like it any better now?'

'Is that a sarcasm?'

'Honestly, no.'

'I do like it better now. A minute ago I was even thinking a very odd thing – that just here would be a marvellous place to build a house.'

She laughed. 'It's one thing to build a house, another to live in it! Now *I* often think that when I'm really old and feel eccentricity finally getting the better of me, I'll come up this way and settle down in peace and be the Biddy Early of my day. You remember the awful stories they used to tell us when we were kids about Biddy Early, the witch who lived round here?'

'Yes, I remember.' He shuddered. 'I expect the old horror haunts the neighbourhood! I'm not so sure about my house!'

'I thought you'd soon find a reason for changing your mind.'

'You're very sure, aren't you, about the sort of chap I am?'

The anger in his voice startled him.

'I'm sorry,' Nell said, looking away from him. 'I have these dreadful schoolmarm habits – I don't seem able to help them.'

Once again he was touched by the gold fringe of her drooping lashes. He did not know how to respond to her apology. He wished he might dare attack her use of words like eccentricity and school marm in reference to herself. In relation to her air and attitude of arrogant beauty they could almost be mistaken for nets of vanity flung out to land a stupendous compliment. And yet he knew that he must not tell her she was lovely, as in this curiously awkward moment he not only saw, but felt, her to be. It struck him that probably with any other woman in the world he would be able to switch away this deadly and disarming moment with immediate flattery or with a kiss.

A kiss! His thoughts checked violently and he forgot his embarrassed silence, plunged into a deeper gravity. To kiss this woman. What an amazing. unpredictable experience! And then he saw the implications of such unforeseen reflection. That he, Matt Costello, should be amazed by the idea of a kiss on no matter what new beautiful mouth, that he should find it difficult to visualise and feel his mind darkening like a boy's before the idea, showed him that he must indeed beware. If things so fresh as fear and wonder could take possession, absolutely uninvited, of a half-dead man –

She turned her face towards him again. She knew her silly comment on herself had embarrassed him, but still she was surprised at the gaucherie that let it fall into a pause. He can be almost as awkward as me, she thought, and then, meeting his eyes, was startled by their darkened, anxious look into forgetting their embarrassment.

'What are you thinking of?' she said.

'May I answer you truthfully?'

She raised her brows.

'I was thinking that if the woman sitting on that rock was called by any other name but Nell Mahoney – I'd, I'd kiss her now.'

A very faint colour rose in her cheeks, but to Matt's amazement she smiled. An innocent, slow smile, without coquetry. He would almost have said that it was a smile of pure pleasure.

'Even with Liam around?' she fenced.

He laughed, thinking as he did so that, Puritan or not, she could produce at the right moment the traditional ease of beauty before emotion.

'Well, no – I had forgotten Liam! Thank God for him!'

'That's an impolite sort of prayer.'

'Don't pretend to misunderstand! If Liam weren't here – '

'Poor Liam! He's been saving us from absurdity all day.'

'If I were to – to try to kiss you, would that be an absurdity?'

Her eyes and voice were very serious as she answered:

'I think so. Because you are in love – with someone in England; and my kisses aren't easily given.'

Liam came bounding up the slope, orchid plants held carefully in his two muddied hands, which he had used as trowels.

'Mother will love these,' he said triumphantly.

'Oh, Aunt Nell, do you think they'll grow at Weir House?'

'I expect so, pet. You must choose a good spot for them.'

'The other side of the river isn't really their climate, I suppose?' said Matt.

'No. Not really. But Daddy says that Mother has green thumbs! Isn't that a funny word, Uncle Matt – green thumbs?'

'We must go home,' said Nell, getting up. 'Everyone will think we're lost.'

Driving back to Mellick the two grownups directed all their conversation back to Liam. Matt was aware that he himself was excessively jocose and knew that such manifestation of nervousness would not escape Nell's observation. But he hardly cared. He was in the grip of astonishment and felt alive and out-of-hand as he had not felt for months. He was excessively grateful to Liam for imposing time and interruption on a new and incalculable tumult. So he let himself go in talkativeness and in comic driving stunts to which the child responded with delight. London was no longer three hundred but three thousand miles away, and the lightning change in perspective was an irrational, intolerable relief. After some hilarious zigzagging on the mountainy track had all but killed a wandering donkey, Matt gave up being funny with the wheel and he and Liam took to singing:

In Dublin's Fair City,
Where the girls are so pretty ...' they sang.

Nell watched him, wondering. But not overmuch. For the moment she felt soothed and careless. And like him, grateful to Liam. She smiled at the singing and, inwardly, at her own vanity which could be so shamelessly placated by what was, after all, an impertinence. 'How commonplace I am,' she thought, 'not to say common.' But there was more relief than embarrassment in the self-criticism.

They drew up at Nell's hall door to find Tom turning his latchkey in it, and a tall priest in the Franciscan habit standing with him on the steps.

'Father Malachi,' said Nell. 'Tom is going to have one of his dialectical evenings.'

Matt, in his role of clever novelist, had often thought that the faint irony with which Nell invariably spoke of Tom had the ring of a tone assumed to substitute, or even to conceal something. Touched by this, but unable to find any deeper symptoms in her of living feeling for Tom, he had concluded that the mannerism, assumed as a shield long ago, when still necessary, was now no more than a habit, and without significance.

This evening, however, the customary lift of amusement in her voice irritated him.

'Poor Father Malachi,' he said with light aridity as he got out of the car.

Liam was on the pavement already, clutching the long parcel of the salmon rod. Matt opened the door of the car for Nell. Tom and the priest surveyed the party from the steps, the former with one eyebrow cocked, and looking a very picture of indulgent amusement.

'What's all this? Are we having a party here?'

'Oh no, Uncle Tom – we've had the party really. We're just leaving Aunt Nell home – with her present! We've been for a lovely drive.'

'A present! Of what nature, Nell, may one ask?'

But Nell, greeting Father Malachi, ignored Tom's insistent eyes.

'A salmon rod,' Matt told him with a cool smile.

'Nell said she'd like one.'

'Indeed? Lucky thing you came home to indulge all our whims for us, Costello!'

'Father Malachi, you haven't met our famous relative,' said Nell, presenting Matt.

The priest stretched out his hand.

'No, and I'm very glad to now. I heard you were around.'

'Naturally,' said Tom. 'A cat can't have kittens in the diocese but our gossiping friar must know. Would you take the risk of dining with a saint of God, Matt?'

They were in the hall now.

'I'd chance it, Heaven help me – but your mother wouldn't think me fit company –'

'My mother lost a shilling at the tables this afternoon, and has therefore, very naturally, retired to bed with a sick headache, so the vegetables will be passed round twice, I'm happy to say!'

Liam giggled delightedly.

'Then *I* could nearly stay to dinner, Uncle Tom, couldn't I?'

'Very nearly – by straining a point.'

'You'll have to, if I do,' said Matt.

But Nell intervened. She felt disposed for the restfulness of an evening with Una, at safe remove from these dart-throwing men.

'I'd like to dine at Weir House,' she said. 'I'll drive you home, Liam, if I may borrow Matt's car?'

She looked at Matt. Tom looked from the one to the other.

'Of course,' said Matt. 'Bring it back in time for me to get home.'

'Oh, you'll find it waiting here when you want it.'

'Is it safe for you to drive his limousine?' Tom asked.

She laughed. 'Really, Thomas! Come on, Liam – let's go. It's after seven.'

'Ok. Perhaps it's better, on account of the orchids. They ought to be planted tonight, Aunt Nell.'

'Ah, a botanical expedition, was it?' Tom descended the steps with Nell and opened the door of the car for her. 'Take care of yourselves in this offensive-looking carriage.'

Nell smiled back to Matt and Father Malachi before she got in. 'I won't do it any harm, Matt,' she said, and as she drove away she asked herself in astonishment why a mood of irrational self-satisfaction had betrayed her into calling Tom 'Thomas,' a thing she had not done since she broke their engagement.

The Sixth Chapter

'Let you go easy with the whiskey, Tom,' said Father Malachi, 'because you know very well that if you loosen your tongue too much we'll have a row.'

'His Reverence and I sometimes come near blows,' said Tom to Matt.

'You'd be well enough matched, but Father Malachi would have the best of it.'

Matt thought that he had never seen a more magnificent man than this monk. He was in his early thirties and as tall and broad-shouldered as Tom, but without an unnecessary ounce of flesh on his body. The ring of dark hair round his tonsured head was curly, his eyes were deeply blue, and all his strong features were in the heroic tradition. He might have sat for Augustus Cæsar in his prime, Matt reflected. Instead he wore a frayed Franciscan habit.

'I'm not so sure,' said Tom. 'There's weight behind my punch. Still, these fellows take such care of themselves nowadays! They're as decadent as the Greeks, by God. Do you know, Matt, what they have now on the roof of their monastery? A tennis court!'

'That's very American of you, Father.'

'Yes, it's a good idea. We have no garden, you see, and the young priests must have exercise.'

'So if a tennis ball, of all things, knocks the eye out of your head in Charles Street one of these days, Matt, you can blame Father Malachi's forehand drive!'

Moths beat about the lamp on Tom's broad desk, and beyond the dark mass of the sycamore tree in the back garden the summer night showed clear and calm. Ice tinkled in the whiskey glasses, and Matt, lighting one of his host's cigars, reflected that Tom Mahoney was the only tolerable kind of connoisseur, one who has no tiresome speeches to make about what he offers, but whose whole personality declares his bland refusal to be associated with the second rate.

Father Malachi neither smoked nor drank and he smiled good-naturedly as the other two adjusted themselves with their creature comforts.

'Yes,' said Tom, smiling too, 'we're as aware all your Reverence that the price of these two cigars would feed an unemployed man for a week – according to recent strange statistics! But we're as callous as the devil, and we're going to smoke them! There's the labour question in Havana, after all.'

'It'd be a hard man that would grudge you your little pleasures, Tom,' said the priest mockingly. 'And I'm not wanting to argue the distribution of wealth. I want to talk to Mellick's returned celebrity.' He turned to Matt. 'Have you come back, like Saint Patrick, "to dwell amongst us"?'

'And preach you a new conversion?'

'To neo-paganism? That would be an enterprise, all right,' said Tom.

'And our friend here might be the very man for it,' said Father Malachi. 'Your books are eloquent and powerful, Matt Costello, and they certainly are "news" to us here in

Ireland, even if news of an unfortunate or unwelcome character.'

'Their being "news" as I think you use the term, Father, is irrelevant.'

'What is the function of such work as yours, I've often wondered?'

'My God!' said Tom, 'you're talking just like my cousin Nell!'

'I'm very much complimented,' said Father Malachi. 'There are few people in this town talk as good sense as Nell.'

'And I hear from Tom that she says my books are "myth-creating, anti-social and unnecessary".'

'You'll forgive me if I say that Nell usually hits a nail on the head.'

Matt laughed.

'It's a waste of energy to hit a nail that's in its place and doing its job,' he said. He was feeling arrogant and cheerful. 'The artist is always "myth-creating, anti-social and unnecessary", in Nell's sense.'

'But you haven't answered the man of God,' said Tom. 'What is the function of your books?'

'Any books, mine or Amanda Ros's or Virgil's exist solely to demonstrate the artist's desire and ability to write them. They are a fruit of the creative function, as irresponsible, if you like, as other fruits of creation. Father Malachi may say what he likes, but men get their children in gratification of themselves, and the Church does not tell them, so far as I know, to pause and consider the chance that the fruits of that "pride of life" may be criminals, murderers, perverters of youth, scandalisers of the little ones. The Church tells them to have their children and stop moralising.'

'It's a sentimental analogy,' said Father Malachi. 'There is a clear faith, a definite duty to God, in the raising of a family.'

'But I allow that, for those who feel it,' said Matt, 'and I am perfectly content that you others don't allow the likes of me our clear faith, our definite duty to – something or other!'

'Ah – "something or other"!'

'Exactly. Something or other. That's as far as I go. I'm not a materialist, because materialism is mere politics, and politics are death to the creative artist. And if Father Malachi insists that I must have a function, a social duty, all right. I believe that now as never before it is the duty of those who can refrain from meddling *not* to meddle. I believe that it is useful at present to be an individual, to be non-doctrinaire. I am not convinced about this, or prepared to be pompous over it – but that may be the very *clou* of its usefulness.'

'You see, Your Reverence, he's as smug as a parish priest!'

'Tom here tells me that he's a good Churchman – and he's well up in Aristotle, whom I haven't read since I left the university. But Aristotle – to whom the Church owes Aquinas – said that poetry is more important than history. I'm not a poet, Father Malachi, but I work in the imagination, and therefore have a chance of being more important than Dev!'

'The shot is too long, my boy! I'm a practical man, concerned with the problem of good and evil here and now, as I think men like you should be.'

'But how could I escape it? It's my stuff – only my terms of reference are individual, not an imposed code. And, as a writer, I prefer the words "true and false". Since my job is not to moralise but to demonstrate.'

'Demonstrate what?'

'That thus and thus, under the glass I use men go about their business. That life is so and so on the screen of my closed eyelids.'

'Closed, you say?'

'Specifically. I speak only for myself when I say that my job is to re-create life, not as it is, good God, but as the peculiarities of my vision and desire assume it. I give you life translated to my idiom. You take it or leave it. But if your leaving it makes me endeavour to force my eyesight differently, or to alter my reaction, then, Father Malachi, I am in danger of committing mortal sin!'

'May God forbid!' said Tom with piety.

The priest laughed deeply.

'A danger you haven't yet encountered, I suppose?' he said.

'I'm warted all over with the mortal sins of a thick skin,' he said. 'I'll certainly go to hell hereafter. So will Tom. If for no better reason than that we sit here smoking and drinking before the generosity of Saint Francis, and haven't a vestige of regret that we don't wear your shabby uniform, or the least desire to emulate you. Oh yes – mortal sins of grossness and greed and comfort loving and turning the deaf ear. Mortal sins of the 'rather-he-than-I' philosophy. But not the Church's mortal sins.'

'You killed men in the patriotic struggle,' said Tom.

'Unlikely. You did, but I was a rotten shot. Anyhow Father Malachi is a patriot, and would call our skirmish "a just war".'

'Most certainly.'

'Well, I'm a pacifist now, Father, and I can't echo your conviction. I don't think there is such a thing as a just war.'

'But His Reverence isn't safe yet, I'd have you know. He's as near a militant Communist as a consecrated priest has ever been – and in the class war that's coming –'

'Is there to be a class war in Ireland?'

'As sure as I'm sitting here,' said Tom. 'And if Dev and the hierarchy go on keeping their heads in the sand it'll be sooner than later.'

'What will you do then, Father Malachi?' said Matt.

The priest was staring at the clear night sky beyond the sycamore tree.

'The Franciscan is the poor man's friend,' said Tom softly, 'and that's not an easy thing to be now, for a man who believes in an hierarchical God. This fellow has been in the head and tail of every strike that has afflicted Mellick in ten years. His sermons are a perpetual embarrassment to his superiors, and he's come mighty near being unfrocked, I'll venture to guess. But in the day of battle, his problem will be solved. They'll ship him off to Madagascar or Patagonia, and by the time he has re-established his power and personality there he'll be old, he'll even be dead. It's easy enough, Matt. Saints are so few and so humble, and the world is wide. His vow of obedience will solve his problem.'

'That's neither true nor fair, Tom,' said the monk. 'And I am not a militant Communist. I am a Franciscan.'

'In other words an anachronism.'

'Not at all. The poor you have always with you, and if Christianity had its way you'd have them more and more. We'd all be what you call poor – levelled down to decent, simple poverty.'

Matt laughed. 'That's impossible now in this too-productive world,' he said. 'On paper at least it should be much easier to make us all rich – levelled up to decent, simple wealth!'

'More's the pity!' said Father Malachi.

'There isn't a chance in a million of things going either way,' said Tom.

'And if there isn't you can mostly blame fellows like Matt Costello,' said the priest. 'It's they who are the instigators and inspirers of egotism, the handers-on of all the romantic and individualist nonsense that's made a shambles of the world –'

'You're not going to blame the arts for being invariably misunderstood, I hope?'

'Artists are dangerous fellows –'

'Plato thought so,' said Tom.

'So does Hitler,' said Matt. 'So does Stalin. So does Dev, I'll be bound!'

'And why not?' Father Malachi asked. 'You use a power you're too proud to explain! You instigate what you cannot possibly control!'

'Control! That's where the world's going crazy,' Matt retorted. 'Oh, that most dangerous word "control"! This abrogation of "control" is the darkest and most hideous arrogance! There's doom in it – nothing else! Who is to control whom, and to what end and by what authority?'

Father Malachi smiled.

'The Church, for instance, is to control its members to the end of their eternal salvation, and by God's authority.'

'And if I believe that and am a contented member of the Church, i.e., if I have the gift of faith, that control works from within me, is a natural part of me, like breathing or talking, and is actually no imposition, but a normal necessity. Ok,' said Matt, 'I am not controlled – I am by nature a member of the Church Militant. But if I'm not so constituted, if I have not the gift of faith, but am none the less what is called sane, and amenable to my own natural moral law –'

'How sure you are of your natural moral law!'

'Oh, Jansenist!'

'Or is it Manichæan?' said Tom.

'Let *me* alone for a minute,' said Father Malachi. 'I'm attacking you – the novelist, the myth-creator. Take emotion, human love, which has given us priests and moralists so much to worry over. It's your particular field, Costello. You examine and present it with unquestionable skill. But you're wasting your time – all you gentry have been doing so for thousands of years – on a non-reality. Romantic love is an invention – the biggest and most dangerous invention of you artists. It isn't in nature at all. It isn't real. It's a trick, an imposition, a thing grafted on –'

'So is divine love, Father Malachi. So is mysticism. So is the belief in the hereafter. And great crimes have been committed in their names too. But that doesn't matter. Humanity must be allowed to take its risks. "Ripeness is all". And romantic love is not an invention so much as a discovery, like America or radium. It's an expansion of life's latitude and possibilities. There's always danger in such discoveries, but Heavens, why not? And those who don't want to explore are not obliged to.'

'You really find it worth your close examination – this same old business of attraction and repulsion? There are so many other forces and beauties in human life –'

'Of course there are. But life is short and industry limited. I take the emotional life of adults for my field as a zoologist might take parasitic worms for his or a surgeon the abdominal zone. To understand my own subject at all means naturally a great deal of general observation of human behaviour, but emotional growth – and decline – is my quarry, and what moves me most to write is a sense of the chasm that roars between our complicated everyday life and the still more complicated life of the breast – yes, and the bridges we fling across, and fail to fling across.'

'All very fine – but these romantic researches are useless – they are unscientific. At their best they are no more than imaginative truth.'

'No more than imaginative truth! My God, what more do you want from the imaginative writer?'

'He wants exemplary deductions from that truth, my boy,' said Tom. 'An edifying synthesis, I suppose –'

'Anything that comes off in literature *is* a synthesis,' said Matt. 'But what do you mean by "edifying"?'

'You take your vocational attitude rather far,' said the monk good-naturedly. 'You knew when you were a schoolboy what we mean over here by "edifying". Does being a writer release you from being an Irishman and a Costello?'

'No. It merely governs those parts in me.'

'And you have no duties to them?'

'None, I think, that could over-rule my duty as a writer – that after all, Father Malachi, is the state of life to which it has pleased God to call me!'

'He has you there, Malachi! He remembers his theology!'

'Not at all. He has merely invented a sentimental sort of Protestant conscience to take the place of the orthodox one he was given at baptism.'

'I haven't "invented" anything. What I am is me. I was a doubter, Father Malachi, and an exerciser of private judgment, long before I was confirmed.'

'You resent our censorship of you, I suppose?'

'I resent the censorship, lock, stock and barrel.'

'Why?'

'Because it is a confession of failure. It is a denial of human judgment and understanding, and a gross intrusion on liberty. If you, Tom or Nell Mahoney may read my books and sit in judgment on them – by what right do you decide that it is not for others to do so? Sheer impertinence – and an example of that fatal tendency in all modern government to level down, not up. In any case, too many negative regulations are a symptom of weakness in any authority. Man is born free –'

'You're as sentimental as Rousseau,' said Tom.

'If I am, that certainly doesn't worry me.'

'Shall we save him, Tom?' said Father Malachi.

'Save him for what?'

'For old Ireland, man! For usefulness and continuity and the Catholic standards in general.'

'Will is attending to all those,' said Matt.

'But you're a man of gifts – and Ireland throws away too many of you without a struggle.'

'Oh well, neither Ireland nor I can have it both ways. I'm not prepared to be saved on Ireland's dictated terms. Why not save Tom?'

'But Tom is here, and saved. There isn't a village of sentimental corruption in that cynic.'

'*Credo quia absurdum,*' said Tom. 'For God's sake, Malachi, have a cigarette or a lemon drop, or something!'

'All right, I'll have a cigarette.'

Tom refilled his glass and Matt's.

'He's an emotionalist, this writer,' the priest said to Tom. 'He could be saved through his emotions.'

'If they weren't already given to the Egyptians,' said Tom.

Matt and he exchanged careful glances. Father Malachi looked from one to the other with mild amusement in his eyes.

'Are you sure of that, Tom?'

'My dear Father Malachi, there's no fool like a sophisticated one.'

'Yes. That occurred to me, too.'

'How do you mean?' Tom asked with sudden sharpness.

The priest did not answer him. 'You two are old friends?' he queried blandly.

'In the easy sense,' said Matt.

'We've had no occasion to test things,' said Tom. 'Old association is not friendship.'

'No, not for toughs like you, I suppose,' Father Malachi mused. 'What are you listening to, Tom?'

'Nothing. Nell going upstairs. That means that your car is intact, I suppose,' he said to Matt.

'You have good ears,' said Matt.

'Oh, he ought to know that footstep,' said the priest.

Silence fell. Matt thought of Nell ascending the long staircase. She would seem ghostlike in the shadows. 'He could be saved through his emotions ... for continuity and the Costello standards ...' Oh, innocent Father Malachi, what safety is there in a sexual impulse, in the resuscitation of the pride of life and the lust of the flesh? What is there good or honourable in the sweetness of revenge or in egotistical victory?

Matt felt suddenly depressed. Three hundred miles away Louise was at this moment playing the last passages of his last act, making those desolate, relentless speeches of flight which, fluttering hints and stabs throughout the play, here rose to tragic declaration. Blind departure, fear, refusal. The sense of senselessness, of all to be done again, of vagueness, folly and enchantment in a mere and selfish mortal, of pain that must be taken and the poison of pity. Of cowardice angelically masquerading. Much ado about a stupid, stony heart. A bitter, unexplained, romantic sketch of a romantic's despair. A play written out of the writer's great first happiness, written in the terror of joy's inspiration and very bitter therefore, as a superstitious immolation. And played – ah, let the world judge if she could play or not that sad caprice of his! Well, and of what use was such achievement, his or hers? Let this Franciscan say. *He* served his time with news of the love of God, insistence on it, and example in himself of how complete reliance on it could kill those common urgencies and greeds which make a hell of life. He preached resignation here and spiritual rest in return for the comfort of an idea, if you like, an illusion. Matt's contribution was a cheaper glamour – a counterirritant of restlessness against restlessness, a denial of patience, an insistence on the full pain, sensation, risk and uneasy bliss of here and now, in return for sensing it, in exaction – and payment – of chance-taking. An idea too with comfort in it – an illusion certainly. But better than sleep, better than death-in-life. Death will come – but in its place. Meantime – an idea, an illusion. And Tom, urbane and scrupulous professional man – he gave a fig for men's conceptions and spiritual needs, and was content to obtain for them plain, common justice. In return for fees, he would add with truth. He and Tom both served life, if they served it at all, to get a living. And the priest, allowing him nobler motives too, worked for the good fee of escaping the struggle for fees. Too proud to fight. I will take a vow of poverty and the Lord will be my shepherd. I shall not want. So, disposing courageously in himself of a major source of vileness, he could smile at whiskey-drinking novelists and lawyers. But all three of us, said Matt, are in a sense in the same case, playing our own hand, and Tom is the most plainly useful. Father Malachi has to prove so much besides to prove his usefulness, and I can prove nothing, nor do I want to.

Usefulness and continuity. These pompous words had no value save in the pleasure they gave the man who believed himself to be promoting them. Their point was subjective – and escapist, like Matt's work. Tell Will that all his solid structure of wife and children and honest toil was an escape, a bolt-hole, and watch his baffled face! But let that be. The thing was that it served. Will was happy and created happiness. No nonsense in that. That was contributory. Would the 'Open Sesame' work for another? Could Will's brother create happiness, on Will's fine-sounding passwords?

Matt had startled himself by threatening to kiss Nell that afternoon. But self-confidence, though half regretting the cavalier impertinence, had instantly acknowledged the validity as well as the implications of the impulse. Matt might announce to a Franciscan that as a writer he overrode all the Irishman-Costello business in himself, but he understood very well that in Ireland one does not threaten to kiss an Irish lady – and let it go at that. And clearly the man who made overtures to Nell Mahoney must be one of two kinds – either an alien who did not give a damn for her out-of-date code and who, desiring her beauty, admitted no barrier against a possibility of mutual pleasure, or an Irishman who knows that he must face the long consequences now, should he desire the perfect flower of that kind of woman, over-civilised, over-controlled, that his male forbears had insisted on.

Matt did give a damn for her out-of-date code, which was her essence, the poignancy of her attraction. In one sharp second of blinding appreciation of her as she sat under the withered hawthorn tree he had seen why instinct drove him crawling home to Mellick when the last blow struck. It was to encounter this farewell. It was to face this major operation that might or might not work. To pay court to Nell Mahoney was the only real way to say goodbye to all that had happened to him, all that he had built up and sought to make himself, all that had been proved and culminated in Louise. Well, the proof had broken down. The culmination had been invalid. The only help now was in dismissal and cutting-off. And here was the test of his intention. He must take it. He must attempt this most extraordinarily dangerous thing in which every inch would be a battle, every idea a dispute. Success in what he now envisaged would mean a fight for every sentence of his future work, and would even mean the risk of surrender to an entirely new and improbable source of inspiration. Success here with her would mean conflict. Goodbye to the Muse, to the paradoxically prompting echo. Goodbye at last, Louise. And he chuckled suddenly, thinking of the gladiators' salutation to Cæsar.

'What's the joke?' said Tom.

'Oh, it's complicated. For all I know it may be on you.' He had a persistent desire to irritate Tom tonight.

Father Malachi raised his brows.

'Now, how could that be, I wonder?'

'No such thing as a joke on Tom Mahoney?' said Matt.

'They don't often come off,' said Tom.

'You two are on each other's nerves tonight,' said Father Malachi. 'No wonder, of course.'

'It's the first time I've noticed Your Reverence being – coquettish,' said Tom.

'Well don't accuse me of being it if I say what's just being going through my head – that it's an odd thing to see two such self-willed and prosperous men still unmarried.'

'Commend me to the chaste for that kind of meditation!' said Tom.

'Why should self-will be an aid to marriage?' asked Matt.

'And anyway, why should we be married?'

'For no more startling reason than that I think you'd make good husbands and fathers.'

'Well, of course if you could let us have that in writing –' said Tom.

'Oh, I daresay you'll both get married pretty soon,' Father Malachi went on musingly, 'only it would be a pity if you got in each other's light over it, or had a disagreement –'

Matt had felt all through the evening that such sudden odd innuendoes from the priest were a puzzle and irritation to Tom, and that in fact they were out of character. But he himself was convinced that they were deliberate, and that the utterance of them was an embarrassment but also some kind of self-imposed obligation for Father Malachi. He said nothing now. He was a stranger. Whatever the priest was trying to say – and surely it was plain? – was meant for Tom. Sentimentalist, playing the warning friend. But Tom, the arrogant, had had twelve years of opportunity.

'Unlikely,' he was saying suavely. 'We don't mix in the same world. Matt has climbed. He can hang up his hat in ducal houses now.'

'Indeed? I didn't know.'

'For God's sake, Malachi! Don't you read your Castlerosse?'

'My what? Good Lord, it's twenty past eleven, and I have to say Mass at six-thirty in the morning.' He stood up and they with him.

'I'll give you a lift, Father,' said Matt.

'Don't bother. I suppose you want to stay and make a clubman's night of it with Tom.'

'No, I don't think so.'

'Matt and I aren't as expansive as when we went to jail together. But that's only natural,' said Tom with an ironic lift of one brow. 'You'd be surprised at how dull we are when we're left alone together, Malachi. Old soldiers may never die, but they certainly fade away.'

'There isn't much fading in either of you yet, but perhaps that's what makes you dull, or careful, with each other.'

They were in the hall now.

'Your conversational style tonight is as novel to me, Your Reverence, as that of my mother's lady friends.'

'Ah, they talk to us poor friars, you know – those excellent ladies, it's our job to talk to them – and the dyer's hand, Tom –'

'Well, look out for your common sense then, because it seems to be in jeopardy.'

Matt's car was parked against the kerb.

'Good night, Tom,' he said and got in and started the engine.

'Sixteen years since you last saw Tom?' mused Father Malachi as they drove through the town.

'Well, I don't suppose he's changed very much. He was born grownup, I'd say.'

'Yes, I think he was – up to a point.'

'Peculiar fellow – but very good. Ought to have been married years ago. But he has a stiff neck, the fool. A very stiff neck.'

Matt said nothing. He was bored by this hymn to Tom Mahoney.

'All the same, though he doesn't deserve it, I'd like him to have his luck in the end. I'd like Tom to be lucky. I'd hate him to be upset.'

Matt drew up outside the Priory in Charles Street.

'I don't know what you're worrying about,' he said stiffly. 'It's always been impossible to upset Tom Mahoney. Good night, Father Malachi.'

'Good night, Matt Costello. Thank you for the drive, and for putting up with my attack on your work.'

'Oh, that!'

Matt drove on, smiling. Attack on your work! This priest whom he had liked and thought impressive had ended up by irritating. He was in a mood of violence and excitement. He let the car fly along the shining road.

THE SEVENTH CHAPTER

Matt was helping Una to do this and that odd job in the herbaceous border. That is, he stood by and held things while she snipped and clipped at her flowers, which graded up from pansies and pinks through stock, columbine, lilies and Canterbury bells to hollyhocks, sunflowers and late, lingering azaleas. A brilliant parade. It was the last Sunday of June.

'I hate delphiniums,' said Matt. 'Delphiniums and lupins bore me to death.'

Una looked affectionately at hers.

'Why on earth?'

'I just think they're bores, Una. Like your parish priest the other night –'

'Anything less like a lupin than poor Father McCarthy –!'

'All bores are alike. I hate yellow flowers, too, except sunflowers and – as a concession to sentiment – primroses.'

'But daffodils, Matt?'

'Oh, I like them coming before the swallow dares and all that – I'm not inhuman – but I would prefer them not to be so damn yellow. If I ever have a garden, Una, there'll be none of your boring old delphiniums and nothing yellow, I think, except a prize-winning display of sunflowers. There's a place in Suffolk, a pub – yes, Una, in England pubs are respectable. They're nice country hotels where the respectable conduct their illicit love affairs at weekends –'

'God forgive them!'

'You hypocrite.'

'Do you mean that I have illicit love affairs?'

'Hardly. But you're not shocked. This "God forgive them" smokescreen behind which sophisticated Ireland chooses to live! At this pub in Suffolk, Una, the sunflowers are as big as plates. They're like enormous dishes swinging in the air. Most amusing.'

'Ridiculous. Things shouldn't be out of proportion.'

'Oh yes, they should if they can. Take Picasso's women.'

'Rather you than I.'

'That's a more *risque* joke than you think, Una.'

'Maybe. And who's Picasso?'

'A painter. Yes, here's some more bast – wait a minute, it's a bit tangled. Flowers are best when they're white or red or pink or purple or navy blue.'

'Navy blue?'

'Like those pansies there. Or some irises.' He looked away towards the beech tree and the garden chairs. 'Will's completely absorbed. Naylor's horoscopes, do you think?'

'Garvin more likely. Will's worried about Knockabree Belle. She's his best milker and a lovely cow.'

Will had been up most of the night with a sick animal, and the vet had called in the morning – but he was himself a far better vet than the professional. It was the day after the purchase of Nell's salmon rod, and Liam had hoped that he, Nell and his father might have gone upstream from the Weir and conducted the first lesson, but Will would not go so far from the cowshed, and some demonstrations of technique on the lawn had had to suffice. Nell, Liam and Maire had now gone for a walk, and were going to attend Benediction at the little parish church on the hilltop. Matt had said that he would collect them in his car.

'Will is marvellous with sick creatures, animal or human,' said Una. 'He's really inventive and helpful in illness. He'd have made a good doctor.'

'Yes, he would. So should I, I think.'

'Oh, you'd have been some kind of flashy specialist in Harley Street, but Will would have been a marvellous GP.'

'Thank you, and I wish Harley Street heard your use of the word "flashy".'

'You're in a good humour today, Matt,' she said tentatively.

Matt felt relieved that good humour was the harmless outward sign of an inner condition of stormy excitement and anxiety. He smiled non-commitally at Una.

'You're happy in Ireland?' she asked. 'You're thinking of staying a long time?'

'Oh, my dear hostess, am I a nuisance? Am I eating too much?'

'Not a nuisance, but a downright bad influence! All these presents and extravagances and perpetual pleasure-seeking!'

'Really, Una! In Mellick!'

'Yes, pleasure-seeking. It's not merely destroying the children and turning them into absolute little cadges, it's ruining me, too! I really don't know what we'll do, we'll be so bored with normal farmhouse life when you go. But perhaps you'll stay. Perhaps you'll buy a house and show us poor benighted gardeners how to grow sunflowers as big as dishes.'

'Perhaps. I – I don't know, Una.'

She thought that for all his amiable fooling with her he really looked tired today. His face was very white and there were shadows of anxiety about his eyes. Now as he gazed southward over the lovely, undulating land of his fathers, his sister-in-law felt stirring in her own breast some of the uneasiness that troubled his face.

'Sean O'Faoláin stole the true word for this countryside, Una,' he said. '"That sighing land" he calls it. I grudge him the phrase. I was born here and he wasn't. I should have said it first.'

'"That sighing land"' She looked about her. 'I don't know. You writers go in for being absurdly sad. You, Matt, for instance. You're very amusing company when you like, and every now and then in your books you're great fun. I know I'm absolutely ignorant about writing, but I really think you're at your best when you're being amusing. Why must you be in the main so wretchedly sad?'

'Because life observed as a whole is wretchedly sad.'

'I haven't found it so.'

'Nor perhaps in the main have I, for myself. But when we write we are not in the commonplace sense ourselves, Una. We seek the universalisation of conceptions sprung from the particular – and for me, when I write and seek to escape the inessentials of myself, the main reflection left in me from life is sadness. Its point, its beauty, its comedy are all dependent on sadness – which has, if you like, nothing to do with me as a man, but masters me as a writer. I'm not being clear –'

'No, not very. I have. a happy life –'

'I know.'

'And I cannot see why millions of others –'

'Millions of others are slaving, Una, or workless, or homeless, or fighting in some brutal army for brutal ideologies they don't even begin to understand, or wasting in prisons because they resisted such ideologies, or hacking coal out of death-trap mines, or working overtime on incendiary bombs, or ranting away in manic depressive wards because they should never have been born –'

'But these things needn't be. No decent person wishes it to be so –'

'Don't they? Anyhow, so things are. Therefore life is sad, no matter how happy you or I may be. It is much more sad than funny, however good our jokes. So when a writer sits still to write – and forget his excellent lunch and the many excellent jokes he heard during it – no matter even if his theme is no more than a lot of upper middle-class fuss about who goes to bed with whom – the main thing that he hears when he settles down in quiet to collect his thoughts, is sorrow. That is the undertone and overtone, that is the only true residue from any set of experiences, and in so far as a writer re-creates its cadence – no matter what his plot-nonsense – he is right. He is reproducing something of the truth if his rhythm insists on sadness. Even if he's not so bloody good a writer, even if he's only sentimental, the rightness of his hearing in that one general thing redeems him somewhat from vulgarity. It hardly matters how flippant a writer is now, or how sloppy; the thing is, he mustn't be so dumb as to be merry.'

'But if being "merry" as you call it, does some good?'

'Oh, that's as may be. But doing good, as usually meant, Una, isn't a writer's prime function.'

'So I gather,' she said mischievously. 'Anyway, Matt, all these theories of yours depend on your mood of the moment, I've noticed.'

'Naturally. What would you have them depend on? And they're only my theories. Why do you egg me on to bore you in this way?'

'I don't know. Your face worries me sometimes. Here, hold this stake a minute, will you?' He held the stake while she tied back a flame-coloured lily. 'I wonder if you'll ever get married?'

'I'd like to,' he said, in a manner so downcast and uncertain that Una was touched – and reminded of Will in trouble.

She did not know how best to proceed with the conversation. During the later weeks of his stay she had concluded that, were he paying court to Nell, marriage between them would not be desirable or productive of happiness. Too many adjustments of temperament and belief would be necessary, adjustments which Nell could not and he would not make. Each was as obstinate and as clear-headed as the other. It would never do. However, Matt was courting no one, and with relief, and regret at the certainty of her relief, Una had dismissed her uncertain match-making plan. It was a pity. It would have been a brilliant and amusing fate for Nell, who was fit to be the wife of a man of letters. Will's brother too – and so nice. Sensitive and generous like Will. But by no means as easy to manage, Una guessed. Would never have been as easy, even had he stayed at home and remained an orthodox Costello. Well, that was that. He wasn't looking for a wife; Nell was in no immediate danger of an unhappy marriage. And still Una felt something in the air. There was something, which was absolutely nothing, about Nell in Matt's presence that arrested, and entirely evaded, Una's intuitions. She knew her sister well, through the impalpable subtleties of affectionate reserve. Nell and Una had never exchanged a serious confidence in their lives and did not foresee that they would ever do so. Although in childhood they had shared a bedroom, then and since then they were shy of even the smallest accidents of physical intimacy and avoided them with rigour; they never exchanged more than the most strictly necessary and superficial information about such bodily ills or indispositions as came their way; they never discussed emotional matters or religion save lightly, and in the presence of others. But they loved and reflected upon each other, and were much concerned for each other's wellbeing. They were typical Irish sisters, in fact. And lately, observing her sister with Matt, noting the almost exaggerated coolness and clarity of the grey eyes as they met his, Una felt repeatedly something that to this day, fantastically enough, she sometimes apprehended when Tom was about – that on this ground Nell was vulnerable, that here she was in danger, and could be hurt. Una could neither account legitimately for this sensation nor experience it without distress. It was nonsense and it saddened her.

Last night, when Nell brought Liam home in Matt's car and stayed to dinner, Una had felt quite foolishly troubled. The girlishness of her sister's mood, her almost irresponsibility, as becoming as it was indefinable, was queer, Una thought. And there was Liam's garbled story of a salmon rod and of Uncle Matt seeming to change his mind about whom it was for, and that anyhow now it was Aunt Nell's. Nell only seemed amused by Liam's reports of the afternoon, and was quite inconsequent in her comments. And looking downright pretty too, by Una's standards. Much less of a *femme fatale* last night than a pretty woman!

Then today there was Matt being curiously friendly and guarded and one-of-the-family, but looking as strained and unrested as poor old Will, who had been up all night. And Nell, arriving to lunch, exaggeratedly her normal self, very cool and white, and heavenly-graceful in a severe, silky dress which Una had not seen before.

There were two things which Una envied Nell. One was the extravagance which her free spinster state allowed her to exercise about clothes. Dress talk bored Nell so much that Una had seen her shut her eyes – keep them most insolently shut while other females thrashed the familiar topic. But she never wore anything which did not fit her as if a part of herself, or which was either ordinary or what is called 'striking'. She usually left Ireland for a part of each vacation, and returning, handed her shopping bills to the Customs officer at Dún Laoghaire without a blink. He may have blinked sometimes, Una thought, for though Nell never looked 'grand' anyone could see that none of her clothes came off the peg. She never seemed to buy as much as a suspender-belt in Mellick, which Una said was both snobbish and unpatriotic. But Nell smiled at that. 'I take the consequences of my vice,' she said. 'I pay the Customs what they ask.' And Una could only give in with, 'Well, I suppose if I had your figure ...', for that was the second thing she envied her younger sister. But she had her consolation. Every now and then she confided quietly to her mirror that plump she might be getting and sylph she never was, but she liked her own face, liked it better than Nell's.

Here then today was Nell, composed, normal and in a new dress, and here was Matt, being very pleasant and looking like death and suddenly bending his head and seeming positively pathetic; but both behaving beautifully on the whole, and almost ignoring each other – and Una carried a persistent sense of waiting and malaise. Absurd. And yet, walking to the farm to see Knockabree Belle with Will after lunch, seeking the reassurance of common sense, she had said to him lightly:

'Would you say Matt has anything weighing on his mind today?'

'I would,' said Will.

'Oh!' said Una.

Further up the lane she tried another shot.

'I thought Nell was in a queer mood at dinner last night.'

'So did I,' said Will. 'Oh, damn my lovely Belle! I wish I knew what to do for her!'

Una was exasperated. She hadn't wanted corroboration. But the worst of Will's sensitiveness was, as she had often noticed before, that it functioned.

'Really, Will,' she said impatiently, 'you ought to have been a woman.'

'I'm glad I wasn't,' he said. 'Being your husband suits me fine, darling.'

Now she stared at Matt, surprised by his air of childish sadness. But he recovered himself in a second, and straightening up, lighted a cigarette.

'I wouldn't be any good at it,' he said gaily.

'Children and all that.'

'Children are nice.'

'Sure they are. So nice that they ought to have absolutely nice parents. That reminds me – you're not selling Liam, are you?'

'No, we're not selling Liam. Do you think him the flower of the flock, Matt?'

'They're all marvels. Only he's of a suitable age for me. I like them best when they can hold a knife and fork and use the nominative pronouns correctly.'

'We'll have another child before Christmas,' Una said.

'Oh, Una! Are you glad?'

'Very glad.'

'Six! My Heavens!'

'Don't be silly. Why not six? Why not twelve?'

'No, Una. Not one more than six. Do you hear?'

She laughed with deep amusement.

'You're very ridiculous, Matt.'

'But it isn't fair to them – to exhaust yourself, to grow ill and old –'

'Do I look ill and old?'

'If you have twelve –'

'I won't have twelve, I expect. But if I did – Anyway, I hate hard-and-fast rules.'

'But look at us. Seven of us grew up – there were ten originally, I think – to find both our parents dead at the moment we most needed them. No money, and no real love from the elders to direct us. Look at the result. Will and I have got something worth having out of life. The others –'

'You're not going to tell me your Jesuit brother has got nothing out of life! And who are you to decide that your sisters have got nothing, or would have been better unborn? Or for that matter, the brother who died in France? It's not like you to be so cocksure and materialistic, Matt! Life is worth living, on most terms.'

'Oh, Una, I wonder! That's a conviction of the sheltered, and you've always been sheltered.'

'Maybe. But it's a conviction anyhow.'

'You're almost alone in it now.'

'Not in Ireland. We're still Catholics here, you know, and believe that man is a spirit, and that it is our duty to go on propagating him to the glory of God.'

'Yes, you're still Catholics – but in the middle class already with a difference. Look about you, Una. Count up any other young families of six you know.'

She smiled graciously in defeat.

'Well, everybody's business is their own. I can only mind mine.'

'That's right,' said Matt. 'Which kind of child are you hoping for this time?'

'Oh, a girl!'

'Why?'

'I'd like to have a raving beauty of a daughter.'

'You have two already.'

'Don't be so correct. Una Bán looks like being lovely – but Maire is plain. You know she is.'

'I know nothing of the kind.'

'Oh, Matt! The poor child *is* plain. It's most unfair – because look at the boys with their unnecessarily lovely faces! And she really is a nice kid – though I know she bores you. You know, Matt, when I consider the bland insolence of men, creatures like you and my cousin Tom, I could die of guilt towards Maire for having made her plain!'

He laughed delightedly.

'Of all the nonsense!'

'It isn't nonsense. It's a fearful thing to be a downright plain woman – unless you're a saint or a genius. And I honestly see no hope of Maire's being either. But perhaps this new child will be perfect!'

'What would you call perfect?'

'Oh – a figure, well exactly like Nell's, I think, and a face – like Helen of Troy!'

'Liar! You mean a face like your own! A lovely open rose of a face. Would you like her to have any sort of a mind?'

'Not much. Not as much as Nell, but a bit more than me.'

'Una, she's going to be an interesting niece. Hurry up and have her quickly.'

'But say she *is* like that, I'll be old, perhaps I'll be dead, when she's perfect.'

'Rubbish! You'll be fifty-four when she goes to her first ball. And people will say, "No wonder she's marvellous! Look at her mother!"'

'Poor child! And even if she *is* marvellous, what good will it do her?'

'It will do her the good of having been marvellous, come what may. There's nothing like it for a woman. To have been beautiful is the thing, hot or cold. Meantime I hope that a future International wing-three-quarter, or Archbishop of Dublin isn't having the laugh of us this minute, Una!'

'Really, Matt,' she said shyly. And then, 'Isn't it time you fetched them home from their devotions?'

'Yes, I think it is. I'm glad I was able to be so useful. Do you think you'll manage to do a little work now without me?'

'I think so. God help those sunflowers of yours, Matt! You'll be a queer sort of gardener.'

'That's what I think, too. *Au revoir,* Una.'

Matt drove through twisting lanes to the little stone church on the hilltop. Cow parsley foamed against the car; the evening sunlight almost dazzled him. When he pulled up by the churchyard he heard the screech of a harmonium. He went into the chapel and stood near the door by the holy water font. The place was full and many men were standing near the doors. Catholic churches are always full for services, he reflected. Drive through Ireland or France on Sunday morning and see the overflow of devout crowding the porches, kneeling on the courtyard flags. How many hundred million believing Catholics were there in the contemporary world? He remembered what someone in Bloomsbury had said to him in disparagement of one of his novels which dealt with a problem of the Catholic conscience: 'It's esoteric, Matt; it's a book written by an Elk for the Brother Elks.' A singularly ignorant comment, he had thought at the time, lacking in sense of history. Now he smiled, edging for room and breath in the singing press of men. Like it or not, Catholicism was not a secret society. Bloomsbury – now that was an esoteric entity. It might indeed have the truth in its beard – who was to say? But it certainly was an Ancient and Venerable Order of Elks.

Rosary and sermon were ended, and the acolytes were lighting candles for Benediction. Our Lady's altar was a blaze of candles. She was a blue-and-white figure with a golden crown, and her foot was on the serpent's head.

Matt could see Nell, kneeling in a bench halfway up the aisle. Shady hat, slim shoulders. Liam's silky head to the left of her; Maire's mushroom straw and daisy-wreath bobbing about on her right.

He knew the hymn which the congregation was singing; it recalled bright May mornings at school when he had sung it as shrilly as no doubt Liam sang it now. But he could not identify that eager soprano voice, for the men about the door sang well and deeply from their chests.

> Do thou, Bright Queen, Star of the Sea,
> Pray for the wanderer, Pray for me.

Matt let his eyes rest on Nell's distant shoulders and realised with anguish that the only thing that was not possible was the only thing there was for him to do. If he could pray now!

For twenty-four hours he had had, as Will and Una guessed, something on his mind. It was a curious weight, which ought to have been a lightness. Knowledge of what he wanted – exact knowledge.

He was hoist with his own petard. He saw that. He had always preached chance-taking and the romantic, reckless line. He hated rules of thumb, and in life and work his sympathies were given to those who took their struggles with individualistic passion, brought them home to their own breasts and settled them at no matter what cost in relation only to the most obstinate of their truth. He believed in impulse, pursuit and danger; high fences and blind riding; the courage to race life as it flies. It was because of all these faiths that his greatest faith was in personal liberty – a faith that had finally driven him out of the Church, but which made it impossible for him to find any resting-place in contemporary life. Save only in that one great love, which had shown him that a man can be most fully himself alone with passion and its irrelevant, eternal flowers. There he had rested, needing no faith or hope. There he could have waited for death, and smiled at the world's devil dance, doing that world against its will the service of believing still in one or two symbols it could not destroy, and might even need again on some very distant day.

But that love had gone. And going had left him more cowardly and lonely than before it came. Louise, his strength, his fire, had crippled and frozen him in the end. Useless to blame her. She had to choose between two duties, and she chose. She did not understand the injury to him. Having had from their love all the nourishment she needed or could digest, no doubt she believed that for him, too, their love had done its best. No doubt she wanted rest now and was unequal to his sustained exaction. That was natural, and in a month of separation he had come to understand and condone it. But it was not, alas, his case. The miracle that she had been to him was, it seemed, a fluke. She had not really understood it – its depth or her resultant responsibility. He had thought she had, and had felt perfectly safe. He had misread; had mistaken deftness for understanding. What he had felt as impregnable love had been no more than her vain, sweet effort towards it; what he had called imagination had only been her histrionic power to obey and answer his. Her love had been generous, and now was used up. But he had settled his on her for life. The word had taken root in her for him.

So in the panic of loss he had doubled home. He had never thought of doing that before. Then one morning it had seemed the only thing to do. And here, in the decorum of family life, amid the gentle and faintly mocking associations of childhood, all the anguish, all the wrath and woe had slowly turned to mere loneliness. A kind of limping peace. An appreciation even of Louise's dilemma and of her right to choose as she had done. But an appreciation, too, of his own emptiness, his lack of place and purpose.

He had realised even in his first days of pain that it was good for him to be at Weir House. Even in moments when the isolation which its atmosphere imposed on him seemed unendurable, he had appreciated an antiseptic power in the innocent contentment of those around him and the obligation upon him as a guest to sustain in so far as he touched that contentment. To play noughts and crosses with Sean, to argue the 'economic war' with Will, to flirt with Una – while humiliation and longing went over him in repetitive and unpredictable waves; to thread long, miserable thoughts of her with acquiescent gossip about stage celebrities and 'Miss Lafleur'; to play the amusing, suave celebrity to an inner tune of idiotic misery – all that, he knew as he suffered it was good for him. To drink 'long life to *The Heart of Stone*' was good. To read her telegrams before the entire assembled family perhaps was best.

No. Best – and he had not seen it clearly until yesterday – had been Nell's comings and goings. His eyes rested still upon her. This woman who from the beginning had known how to irritate and touch him in one stroke, who was as resistantly as Louise was pliantly sensitive to life, who felt in denial what the other felt in expression. In Nell very strangely he saw a strange, impossible hope.

He did not hoodwink himself. The leopard does not change his spots, and hope and life were ebbing back because she was a woman, and beautiful. The rebound, the commonplace. But it was not that – not so easy. It was not love that was at issue now, but faith. The implacable past froze round the former word. But life stretched forward and imagination was not dead, nor was vitality. Bluebeard might lock a room and expect understanding of Fatima. In return for what? Funnily enough, in return for his faith, and his desperate need of hers. Oh, strengthened by his awareness of her beauty, her sanity, her traditional magnificence. Given her faith in that awareness in him, he need not fail. He could die and be re-born. Here at home, accepted by her swift and acquiescent intelligence, revived by her beauty, he would begin again. The past, however arrogant, is always for its sins the past. Life begins in every new idea. And here was one, most difficult to express, most conceited-sounding and important. Nell, will you take me as I am? For no better reason than that I believe my cure is in you? With no more important purpose than that you would make me self-confident again, and therefore, God help me, happy? Wilt thou, Fatima, take this man, Bluebeard, to have and to hold ...

Matt dropped on his knees and leant his head against the holy water font. Make her say yes. Make her do this ridiculous thing for me. Oh, make her. I have no faith except in her. In all she is, and in our children. Oh, make it happen. Give me the words to make it clear to her. Tonight. Before I sleep again. Tonight. Make her say yes to my impertinence. Make this thing happen.

The men sang deeply round him:

> ... Mother of Christ, Star of the Sea,
> Pray for the wanderer, pray for me.

THE EIGHTH CHAPTER

Will was very happy at dinner. Knockabree Belle had turned the corner, and they must drink to the gallant creature in champagne. 'Poor old girl,' said Una, 'it's she who should be drinking this, not us.'

'In twenty-four hours she's had enough brandy to give Matt and me the d.t.'s,' said Will. 'I don't think she'll be much good again – this attack is probably the end of her heyday – but she deserves a happy old age.'

Matt felt inert, unable to take his usual part in the table-talk. The effort to control anxiety had induced along his nerves a flow of irrational sadness which blurred his wits; a defence mechanism which kept his mind from full panic, but compensatingly made him unable to control the vague tremors which ran across his shoulders and through his arms. His outer brain toiled intermittently, therefore, with the necessity to keep his hands from trembling while he nursed himself in the flux and reflux of this protective mood of melancholy. The reality he awaited might also wait a little on him. So, letting the familiar voices flow, he looked with sentimental deliberation about the room: at his father's equine portraits, at Will's silver trophies, at the heavy-headed roses on the table. The brilliant evening light dramatised everything, making a gilded cloud of Una's head, and giving to Nell's remote, grave face a Fra Angelico exaggeration. And the inertia of sadness increased, became heavy as foreboding. It is such sadness as a man feels in the hour before he leaves home for a hospital and an illness, or as may sometimes choke the heart of a child about to return to school after happy holidays. Irrational, self-pitying – but deadly sorrow. A farewell heard only by the self. A knowledge of inescapable change.

It was a month – thirty days – since he had first sat here and opposite Nell, as now. Then she had exasperated him with her 'superiority' and her faint air of seeming to sneer at everything he stood for; but, lost in the trouble and disillusionment that had brought him hither he had thought himself no more than amused by her resistant coolness. And now – God alone knew by what processes – she was a part of that very trouble, had increased and developed it from a negative into a positive and immediate thing, for which there was, it just might be, a homoeopathic cure. Now he was in her hands and expectant, who thirty days ago had been his own closely guarded concern, and out of reach of expectation. Now it was by that very superiority that he desired to measure his remaining days. Now by an act of faith he proposed to escape from love and into happiness. Now when he had nothing to give he stood to lose everything. Oh, perfect gamble! Oh, ironic, unexpected throw!

'Do have more strawberries, Matt?'

'No, thank you, Una.'

'I will, please,' said Will, who loved strawberries.

Matt lifted his champagne glass.

'Heavens, how your hand shakes!' said Una.

'It does that often when I'm tired. It really isn't alcoholism, Una.'

'You don't look as if it was, old chap,' said Will.

'But I'm sorry you're tired. Your native air ought to do you more good than it seems to.'

'I should be working, like all the rest of you. Idleness tires me terribly after a bit.'

'I thought perhaps you were working,' Nell said, meeting his eyes gravely and with a certain veiled anxiety.

'No,' he said, taking courage from a sense of isolation with her which her look imposed. 'I'll begin soon perhaps. But I must get acclimatised to the mockery of my ancestors.'

'They don't mock you, Matt, I'm sure,' said Una. 'They must love having a famous descendant.'

'Perhaps they boast about you to their cronies,' said Nell.

Matt searched her face for a clue to the particular gentleness he felt in her voice, but nothing escaped past the quick defensive look of shyness which he knew now as her frequent response to him.

They crossed to the drawing room. The children were shouting, as usual, to be visited, and Una and Nell rose immediately after they had gulped their coffee, hurrying to placate them. Matt crossed to the door to open it and followed the ladies into the hall.

'I'm going down to the weir,' he said. 'Will you come down there when you've left the children, Nell?'

'Yes,' she said and half-smiled back to him from the foot of the stairs. He turned then and went into the garden, descending with slow steps to the riverbank.

He waited for her by the stone parapet a little way upstream. He smoked and looked about him with deliberation. The summer day still poured its brilliance on grass and water; birds sang and stirred, dragonflies darted in glory; a salmon came over the weir with the leap of a god. But a bat wheeled too, smells of syringa and woodbine were sweetly palpable and one by one the stars moved into place. Nigh was taking over.

Matt turned on his elbow and looked towards the house; presently saw Nell come out from it and take the winding, downward path which led to where he waited. The western light out of which she came made her seem exaggeratedly dark, unlike herself. He straightened up, and threw his cigarette into the river. Make her understand. Make her say yes and have pity.

'Have they stopped shouting?' he asked as she came up with him. 'Are they asleep now?'

'Except Liam. I don't think he ever sleeps.'

They moved side by side along the path, going upstream.

'Will you smoke?'

He lighted her cigarette and they went on.

'Yesterday, Nell,' he began, 'yesterday – I was rude, I was clumsy.'

'I – hadn't thought of it as rudeness.'

'It wasn't meant as rudeness. It simply was what I meant.' He saw her smile. 'You're thinking that rudeness is often simply what people mean.'

'I wasn't exactly thinking that.'

'Still – it was a clumsy way to begin – with you.'

He spoke as if to himself.

'You're being a little mysterious,' she said gently.

'Am I?' He burst out laughing. 'Oh, but don't you see – I'm on strange ground?'

They had come to a place where the path widened to form a gravelled landing stage, with mossy water steps against which an old canoe was moored. The river curved eastward here and was wide and bright. There was a wooden seat under the hawthorn hedge.

'This used to be the best stretch for swimming, we always thought,' said Matt. 'But now they seem to prefer to go down near Knockabree Bridge.'

They were silent for a few seconds. Nell sat on the wooden bench under the hedge and looked at Matt, who stood on the edge of the landing stage, gazing down into the water. She had no sure clue as to what he had in mind to say to her, save that obviously it concerned the condition of entanglement in which their friendship now found itself, and which his impulsive remarks of yesterday afternoon had exposed. There were two – or three – possible ways that he might take in this conversation, she thought. Harking back rather absurdly to the pre-war Irish tradition of politeness to ladies in which he was brought up, he might think her puritanical standards demanded an elaborate apology and explanation. She smiled at that, though faintly bored by such stupidity. Or, having undoubtedly an air about him, like it or not, which would have made those aunts and grandmothers of 1910, with whom he so obstinately mixed her up, describe him as a 'flirt' a 'ladykiller' – though she knew well enough that 'ladykilling' as its period meant it was not the horse for this man's money – he might, to relieve tedium, amuse himself by trying to get the kiss with which he had threatened her – believing perhaps that such an old-fashioned pastime might amuse and flatter her, and perhaps even finding in her primness a curiosity worth a novelist's examination. Or – it was just possible – his desire for this interview might be quite natural, might prefigure some real exaction.

She was touched by the look of him as he stood there and stared into the water. This appeal that he could make to her when he was off his guard was very definite. He was not tall, like Tom. Five-foot-nine at most – yes, seven inches taller than Napoleon, admittedly, and with power in his threatening heaviness. Less aquiline too, and with a more romantic, less deliberative eye. But heavy-headed and formidable like the Emperor. She smiled at that. Because why should he be so? He was not the Emperor. His writings, the fruit of real talent, and marked by a sober, complicated sensitiveness which was peculiarly his own, were yet no more important than the works of a hundred of his contemporaries, equally talented. He was a man of legitimate gift – by no means an immortal. But as a person he was, curiously enough, behind his façade significant. In personal relationships he could scatter all the largesse of a victor – generosity and joy, belief and inspiration, an exaggerated but from him true and wild appreciation, a passion of burning gratitude. Thus he could be, she was sure, in triumph – his happiness so strong as to be the very source and pledge of its own changelessness for him and its bestower. That was to her the most marked suggestion of his personality – that out of contentment he could make everything grow, but that in defeat, as now, there was paralysis. In defeat he could not live. He was out of his element and stupefied. He could not take dullness normally. For him it was not normal – it was death. For him to be without centre and expression of desire, without fierce personal direction, to be forbidden a magnet north, was to be incapacitated, blinded. In that, she reflected, he was not like other men who could find it natural to be dull, to have no flame within, or without being dull at all could be a kingdom to themselves, and light their own fires. In this visible dependence of his nature on visitation from without he justified his writings as true at least by his own terms of reference. His romanticism, like it or not, was not made up. It was he. Matt Costello. And, having watched him struggle a whole month with paralysis, with the abnormality of non-direction and defeat, it seemed to her that his necessity was now in train to lead him some strange dance – as Napoleon's did on Elba, she thought with benevolent irony.

'What is it?' she said. 'What do you want to say to me?'

'Give me time.'

'Is it so difficult?'

He looked up into the sky.

'Nell, do you like me at all?'

'Yes.'

'You didn't – at first.'

'I didn't expect to, or particularly want to.'

'You made that clear.'

'Did it matter? Anyhow, my manners are bad and I hate strangers – particularly celebrated ones.'

He laughed. 'Are you so shy then?'

'Let's call it that. Really it's conceit and God knows about what. But I hate being submitted to judgment – or ignored.'

He raised his brows. 'Well?'

'I honestly couldn't make out which you were doing to me – and anyway you weren't the sort of person I had expected. And you were preoccupied – and unhappy.'

'Are you happy?'

'If I were speaking seriously I think I'd say "No".'

He began to pace about the landing stage, then suddenly halted and faced her.

'Since you like me a little,' he said, 'that's something! And since you have seen that I'm "preoccupied and unhappy", well, that's something too. Nell, there are words I can't use, there are things I can't speak of or forget, I have nothing really, I am nothing, and I know what you think of my work and my views and my life – but – don't you see? – I want with all my soul to marry you!'

She was amazed. That he should have had such an idea had never once occurred to her – though she had thought of him with reference to love and its consequences. She raised her eyes to him while she searched for an answer, and he was stabbed by their look of bewilderment.

'No, no – don't answer yet. I know it sounds senseless, almost a kind of insult – yes, in a way it's that! Oh, how can I ever explain myself to you, Nell?'

'Try to,' she said. 'You – you really must explain.'

'But I don't want to lose whatever liking you may have for me! Oh well – something happened to me lately that I couldn't endure. I didn't know what to do. I was unable to face being alone with it – and I couldn't stand the chance of meeting ordinary friends, people who have taken recent arrangements of my life for granted. And suddenly I thought of Will and Una and Weir House. Nell, I've been sorry for myself more than once before, and I've had to live down sickening and insulting situations like everyone else, but always, honestly, there used to be a loophole feeling, a kind of satisfaction in believing myself "a wiser man" as they say! It's seemed normal for things to end, even if the moment was not always the right one. I'm talking like a cad, but I must chance that. This time – from beginning to end it was different from anything on earth. It took much more and gave me much more than I could possibly explain, made me a better writer than I had been, and overwhelmed me with ideas and ambitions. Marriage was impossible during the two years I'm talking of. She was married, her husband was out of England nearly all the time, and refusing to divorce her. But I was as certain as that that is the moon that we'd be married within say a year from now. I lived for that certainty which it was impossible not to feel, and which she felt too – until lately. Until he came back and the issue was definite. But marriage or no marriage I was safe, I thought. It always seemed merely the freakish fact that, whatever she or I might do to other people or about things in general, we were somehow unable to butcher each other. That was how it felt – like a funny miracle. It was always like that in the end, about everything. No matter what sort of rows we had. Rows were useless. They did nothing whatever to what we knew and felt. Until she decided, suddenly – during a weekend – that she must say with her husband and give me up. And then rows were more than ever useless – though we had them by the thousand. They explained nothing. This had been, and now by decision it was to be that. There seemed no way of talking sense. Oh well!'

He paused in his pacing about, and lighted a cigarette. His hands shook violently. Nell watched him with compassion. Twilight, deepening, stressed the deep lines of his face. Down towards the weir a belated blackbird was singing.

'If – if Will were to lose Una, there would be no loophole. There would be nothing bearable in such a loss, and he would not be able to console himself with caddish talk about being "a wiser man". And even if you've led what's called a loose life, if you've been a discreditable sort of chap like me, you can be lucky just once, about love. It was like that – and its ending was pure loss. No loophole anywhere. Nothing. It was everything; it made me. And when it stopped, I had no way at all of explaining to myself that I could get on without it. I'm – I'm trying to tell you things exactly,' he said nervously. 'I mustn't exaggerate.'

He paused again.

'Are you cold, Nell?'

'No, it's warm tonight.'

He noticed that she was wearing the jacket of her pale, silky dress.

'That's a lovely colour,' he said. 'You look like ghost sitting there.' He looked away from her again across the river. 'Over here, away from it all, I discovered that I wasn't wrong,' he said. 'I'm not "a wiser man" now, but very much the reverse. All that I've got from a month of this absolute silence – I haven't written to her even once – is acceptance. I never thought I could take a thing like this lying down, but I've had to, and I've taken it. But I can't stay for ever in a funk hole like this. I can't breathe. And neither can I go back to the world I'm used to. She was the climax of all that, its flower and justification, she made it into a very much better thing than itself. Without her, apart from the perpetual reminder, and fear of meeting her, it would be just the old shoddy round it was, and that I was so sick of when I met her. There's nothing in my former life if she is gone. If I'm to live I can't go back that way. And I want to live. Oh, all this – egotism and impertinence! But will you have a little patience still?'

'Give me a cigarette.'

He came and gave her one, lighted it. He stared at her, uneasy for a sign from her still face.

'I want a new life, I do not think I have ever really wanted to commit suicide. I have neither humility nor courage enough, I think. But I don't see myself as a dear old cynic, don't you know, a bittersweet contemplative, a *si jeunesse savait* sort of guy. Living is feeling, being involved and responsible, I think. If I'm to live and work it must be that way. Father Malachi said something good-natured about "saving" me for usefulness, etc. I don't think that a very important job to recommend to anyone else – and I'd like to save myself. And I see a way, and I'm taking a fling at it, my God! I saw it yesterday, Nell, as if it were lightning! I came alive in an extraordinary flash of panic, and I was so scared that I believe I talked like some kind of movie gent!'

She smiled at him and made as if to speak, but he flung out a hand imploringly.

'I beg you to let me say my say. I'm not stone-blind, Nell; I've seen from the beginning that you are extraordinarily beautiful –'

'You didn't like me.'

'At first I didn't care for your sarcasm.'

'Especially when I directed it at – Louise Lafleur.'

'How did you know – it was she?'

She laughed softly.

'Only by looking at your face when her name cropped up.'

This irritated him.

'I've kept her name as much out of things as possible.'

'Yes.'

'So you've known it was Louise!'

'Oh, Matt, one isn't quite half-witted.'

'Had you guessed that first night when you were being so –'

'So unpleasant? I think so.'

'Why were you harsh about her?'

They stared at each other.

'I don't know,' she said nervously. '"Glamour" bores me, I think.'

They were on dangerous ground. He moved away, moved down the steps and kicked at the leaking canoe.

'Rotten old boat,' he said. 'Where was I?'

'That I was extraordinarily beautiful, but you didn't care for my sarcasm –'

'Nor do I now. Oh, Nell, I'm making a fool of myself, I know – but I must!'

'Forgive me – and go on.'

'I will. I didn't care for your sarcasm, but I liked you. Liked you increasingly. Noticed that you are gentle and sensitive and hellishly quick-witted. That you are as graceful as a myth, and as cool as a cucumber! And that you dress with terrifying *savoir faire*.'

'You notice clothes?'

'Heavens, yes. And yours – well, of course, they're only a part of your "caviar personality" as Tom might say.'

'Does Tom say I'm caviar?'

'I believe he has said something of the kind.'

He came up the steps again and to her, halting by the bench. He began to pull nervously at the hawthorn leaves.

'We used to eat these when we were kids. We called them "bread-and-cheese".'

'So did we.'

'You were like that – what you are. Difficult, unusual, beautiful, caviar. I could see it all but – you understand? – it didn't mean a thing to me. How could it?' She spoke softly, almost as if afraid he'd hear her.

'I wish I could hoodwink myself, Nell. I wish I could offer you a heart on the rebound. I wish I could use a lot of art to explain away the immovable. But I can't. I'm offering you nothing, in fact – and I'm asking you for everything. That's my chivalrous plan.'

'Nothing?'

'Listen. If you did marry me, you'd be doing an extraordinary thing. You believe in all the mysteries of the Catholic Church and in its absolute moral authority. You also believe in a whole tissue of minor taboos and obligations and prohibitions which derive from your central belief, and also from being a citizen of Dev's Free State and a victim of the universal *Zeitgeist.* No, let me go on. I believe in none of those things. I think I'm constitutionally incredulous, but that cuts both ways, Nell, because at least I have been unable to hook up with any new *credos,* to take the place of those that forsook me when I was still at school. So, if you married me, you'd be marrying an unbeliever, but one who would naturally abide by the laws of the Church in so far as they affected our marriage and our children. You'd be marrying a writer whose work you dislike and regard as unfit for Irish readers – though you read it yourself –'

'You've never let me explain about your work –'

'I will, one day. If you married me we'd have to fight it out. Naturally, I can give you no pledge about something so entirely my own, but I swear we would thrash it out, and I think it unlikely that if I was your husband I would feel able to publish anything of which you absolutely disapproved. Still, you'd be marrying a writer who came to you without faith or morals – would that frighten you?'

'Yes.'

'You'd be marrying a man who couldn't use the ordinary words of courtship, Nell! You see, I can't, I can't! She did something to my whole idea of love! Oh God, the word is like a graveyard, Nell! Can't you see? Can't you understand?'

'One could live without the word.'

'I wonder. The man who married you should be free with it. He should be single-tracked, Nell, with nothing to explain away or be afraid of.'

'Yes – it seems a minimum, for marriage.'

'He shouldn't be a sick man, anyhow.'

'That's you. A sick man planning to take a cure.'

He turned away from her sharply.

'Yes. God, where did I get the impudence to ask you?'

'What put it into your head?'

'The commonest of all things. Oh God – yesterday when you were sitting under that hawthorn tree and looking distressed about something or other you'd said, I suddenly understood that – I want you! I saw, great Heaven, that it would be amazing, extraordinary – to be your lover!'

Their eyes met now, but she did not speak.

'And when I said something flat and silly about wanting to kiss you – oh, you looked pleased, you looked heavenly!

So then this idea came, this crazy hope! But since I *can't* say simply as your suitor should, "I love you"; since I can't pretend that there is nothing else in me but this desire, or that Louise has ceased to be – you see, I can't court you honourably! I can't word the thing like a gent! I want you – '

'But you want her more.'

'She's over and done with. She doesn't want me and it's finished. If you did marry me, Nell, I'd give you all my trust and faith and gratitude; I'd make a new kind of life with you, here in Ireland, bowing the knee to old Dev! I'd be a good husband, honestly – all the Costellos are! And if you helped me, we'd be happy. But – what happened before I met you has made me what you see, what you would marry, Nell – and it doesn't die.'

'And if you can help it, it never will.'

'Ah!' He paused. 'That's all I have to say for myself, I think. God knows it isn't much.'

He walked to the edge of the water and lighted another cigarette.

It was Nell's cue. She clasped her hands together, wringing her fingers on each other hurtfully. She closed her eyes and beat about her brain for truth. She did not tremble in moments of agitation as Matt did – she had a somewhat exaggerated habit of outward calm – but all the time that he was talking she had been the plaything of a storm, and unable to think. Now she must take hold of herself and speak to him. She looked about her and up to the sky. The stars were many and clear. Cassiopeia hung crookedly above the house. She could see the lighted drawing room windows, and even remotely hear Will singing. Champagne had made him vocal, no doubt. Poor Una, accompanying like an angel while she ached to read Beach Thomas in the *Observer*.

Nell's eyes came back to Matt, who was looking at her.

'I cannot marry you,' she said.

The words astonished her, but did not seem to be a surprise to him. He bent his head in acknowledgment and turned away.

'Let me explain –'

'No, no. Truly, there's no need to. I know it was a most extraordinary suggestion.'

'It surprised me.'

'What did you think I was going to say to you?'

'Something else. I thought you might be going to suggest –'

He turned and stared at her.

'What, Nell?'

'That – that we might be lovers.'

'Great God! How could you possibly have –'

'You have had mistresses? And they have mostly been – like me – what we call "ladies"?'

'Why, yes, but – you, Una's sister! You, Nell – born in Mellick!'

'All women are born somewhere.'

'Of all the preposterous, unlikely notions –'

'Really, you're very like Will.'

He gave a short, hard laugh. 'I suppose so.'

'I wouldn't have consented, Matt – but it would have been a – more honest idea than – than marriage.'

'What do you mean?'

'Oh, does it matter? I couldn't possibly explain.'

'You must.'

'All right.' She lifted her head and began to speak rapidly. 'There's only one thing you're determined upon, Matt – that Louise Lafleur is not to die! You're a great artist and she's your greatest creation. It hardly matters that the woman on whom you planted this superb conception, in whom you proved it, the actress still living and playing in London, has turned out to be exactly what she always was – normal and sensible like the rest of us. Good luck to her – she served your turn, and helped you to establish at last in your own exact terms, and to serve your exactest need, the Illusion you have been pursuing all through life. You have it now – she gave it to you. You know every inflection of its voice, and every peculiar movement of its hands. You have been enabled to believe in the actuality of a fantasy at last made clear. Galatea. It is your justification – and if it were to die, you might as well. But it won't. It lives through you, and never had any essential dependence on her. The artist in you knows all that and is perfectly calm and hard inside, having got away with precisely what he wanted. But the man – the man is lonely and finds this temporary situation dull, is used to pleasure –'

He made as if to interrupt, but she hurried on.

'– and so, being in Mellick where a lady is still what she was in 1912, and finding one of us desirable in some way which fortunately does not threaten the Holy of Holies – you prescribe marriage for yourself, having first erected every sort of fence around the great Illusion! It would be braver and more realistic to take more casual comforts, and chance the draughts. You must pay something for the sweets of temperament. But a wife is just as sacred an undertaking as an Illusion, Matt – and she has sweeping rights.'

He did not answer at once. He moved uneasily about the little clearing, then came and stood before her.

'You aren't quite right,' he said. 'Louise, believe it or not, was such a complete reality, such an isolated certainty that it seems to me that nothing can balance her loss except the establishment of some other complete reality – something absolutely serious. Marriage with you, Nell, life here at home in relation to standards I forsook long ago, children – well, yesterday, and all today, those things have seemed to me a sheet anchor. It was necessary to be honest in asking for them – and perhaps I was pompous. However – you have answered me – with more understanding than I'm worth. You're more or less right about the casual comforts. I know them, and they'll serve. But if you thought I was cheating, I'm sorry.'

'Oh, not cheating me. You've taken great trouble not to do that. But cheating yourself. And I'm not blaming you, great Heaven! I could cheat myself too. I've been very near it tonight.'

'You?'

'God – this vestige of brain I have – it makes an obstacle race of everything. If only I had more – or none!'

'What do you mean?'

'Can't you see? Oh, Matt, if I weren't just a little too intelligent for this situation – I'd, I'd say "yes," I'd marry you.'

He came to her and took her clenched hands. He dropped on his knees beside her.

'Say it, Nell, I beg you, say it!'

'No, I'll never say it.'

'Why?'

She looked straight into his eyes that were now so near to hers.

'Because – because I'd love to.'

'Then, then – but this is cruelty, vindictiveness!'

'No, it isn't. Let go of my hands. I can't think when I'm trapped like this!'

'I won't let go. I don't want you to think!'

'Listen. I'm not in love with you – yet. But it's going that way. I've thought so lately. If I married you, I'd fall in love, I'd love you. But I'm not taking on any mad competition with *her*! I – I hate her already! I hate your voice when you talk about her! I hate the sudden silences you fall into! If I were your wife – oh, you romantics with your insolence! Your determination to have it both ways!'

'But, Nell, if I stayed with you, it was my hope –'

'I'm too old and too quick-witted,' she said wearily. 'I simply haven't the courage. Besides, you don't *want* to forget her. You dread the time when her name won't trouble you, when you'll be hazy about the sound of her voice –'

He saw Louise – in her dressing room, taking off makeup, looking her worst. She was preoccupied, and frowned at her reflection. He could not answer Nell.

'You see,' she said. 'Oh, I'd like to be married, and have children. But if I loved you, I'd have to have all your love. It's the usual bargain – in these parts.'

She pulled her hands away and covered her face. Her shoulders shook.

'Nell – don't cry.'

'Go back to your own world, Matt – you'll find some solution there. There isn't any in Ireland. If – if I were a chance taker, like you! If I were younger –'

'Oh, Nell, don't cry!'

'But then – I bungled things too. That was entirely my own fault.'

'It's a long time ago.'

'Yes. And I remember everything about it – which ought to be a warning. Indeed it has been.'

She stood up, drying her eyes. One hand fell to his head where he knelt and she took his heavy forelock, twisting it about her fingers.

'Napoleon,' she said, and smiled down at him. She looked brilliantly beautiful. He sprang to his feet and caught her hand to his mouth.

'Is there no hope?'

'Oh, Matt, if only you had never seen her! If only she were dead!'

Their hands fell apart and coldness blew between them.

'I must go now. No, don't come with me. I'll go straight to my car and home. Tell Una – oh, anything you like.'

Her voice was shaking again, and he saw tears shining on her face.

'Nell, Nell!' he said. But she was gone. She had vanished along the overhung river path. Presently he heard the engine of her car start up, and heard the car move away along the drive. He listened to its last faraway hum. Then he sat on the bench under the hawthorn hedge and smoked until his cigarette case was empty. The voice of the weir was very loud; he marvelled that they had not noticed it when talking. Soon the lights disappeared from the drawing room window, and were replaced by lights in a room overhead.

The Ninth Chapter

Outside Mellick Nell pulled up the car and made an effort to dry her eyes once and for all, make up her face, and have done with a seizure of self-pity. It was unlikely that she would encounter anyone between her car and her room. Aunt Hannah and the servants would be in bed, and Tom in his study – reading Gibbon, she thought with a smile, as it was Sunday night. 'I am a man of habits, good habits.' She stared at her reflection in her handbag mirror, and decided that even the kitchen cat had better not see her tonight. She did her best with powder and lipstick, combed her hair and lighted a cigarette. As she did so and slowly, reluctantly, put the car into movement again, she reasoned with herself, but with more caution than mockery, for she still felt too unsteady to face her own severity.

Why all these so unusual tears? She was not in love with Matt Costello – that is, if being in love was what she had felt twelve years ago for another. But he had attracted and disturbed her. He suggested a force which, once yielded to, would carry her far and deep in feeling. She would have been glad of that. She was tired of her own aloofness.

She had never wanted the detachment which circumstances forced on her and which her proud temperament exaggerated in acceptance. She had often earnestly wished she could marry one or other of her chance admirers, but her first love had fixed a standard below which she could not stoop. It was not only in clothes that she hated the reach-me-down. There was nothing of that about Matt Costello – and yesterday mistaking the look in his face, she had actually thought that she had beaten the arrogant, voluptuous ghost behind his shoulders. Not finally, perhaps – but for the nonce. She had thought that he wanted the impossible – to have her for mistress. And she had been perversely pleased with him, perversely tempted. She could not have been his mistress. She knew that the price would have been too much – that her Catholic integrity would have been mortally injured by such a surrender to a mood of release and victory – such collapse before the vulgarity, 'sex appeal.' 'Sex appeal' – it was important. When Nell was a young girl her imagination had constantly reeled back from the unsoundable undertaking of marriage, which she beheld her contemporaries snatching at as gaily as if it was a Christmas present or a summer outing. Marriage, to her, seemed exacting beyond the courage granted to humanity. Not so much in its central function as in its ramified implications, the sheer measurelessness of its spiritual, emotional and physical claims. To live as one flesh with another. To her this had seemed a mere flat statement of the impossible. She had looked with amazement into the faces of friends about to marry. But he, her first, indeed her only love, had swept all that away. Loving him she had known that the thing could be attempted. Courage – indeed yes. But it could be done. There was some medicine, or poison, in love which made the rash idea not merely thinkable, but to be desired. Looking back from maturer years to her brief, happy engagement, she had seen that the common contemporary phrase explained it. He had had 'sex appeal' for her. And no one else had had it afterwards – until Matt Costello turned up. She was too old and cautious now to fall in love of her own impetus, or uninvited; and Matt had hardly made a secret of the ghost in his eyes. Nevertheless, he could have captured her love. Even tonight, if he had stopped talking, and kissed her – she stepped with savagery on the accelerator. Good Heavens, a dead man's consolation! How could he possibly dream that I would marry him to be that? And yet, if I had done it, would he not also have been mine? Or my revenge, my sweet revenge. Was that what I've been flirting with? Revenge on whom for what?

She left the car in the street, as she often did on summer nights. As she got out of it she was angrily aware that there were tears in her eyes again, and splashing down her face. She dabbed at them with her wet handkerchief and, turning to the house, saw Tom at the top of the steps. He looked powerful and censorious. A pair of tortoiseshell-rimmed glasses were sliding down his nose, and his fingers were between the pages of a book.

'Ah! So you're *not* stretched out for dead on the Dublin road! But what do you mean by coming up this street like a "round-the-houses" champion?'

'Sorry, officer. Speedometer stuck.'

'And crying too, by God! Crying at the wheel. We'll soon be hiring our chauffeurs from the County Asylum!'

'I'm sorry, Tom. Good night.'

They were at the foot of the stairs now and she started to ascend. But he had her by the elbow and his eyes did not leave her face. Strong light streamed on her through the open door of his study.

'Sorry? Faith, you look it. What are the tears for, in Heaven's name?'

His tone was markedly ironic and she picked it up.

'Mere femininity. Good night.'

He did not let go of her elbow.

'Femininity. That's it. That brings me to my point.'

'Point?'

'Yes. I want to talk to you. Now.'

'It's late.'

'You can sleep tomorrow.'

'I can't. There are still three days of exams before the end of term.'

'You needn't attend.'

She pulled away from him.

'Really, Tom, I'm tired.'

'You look it. You might as well stop arguing, Nell. I've things to say, and I'll say them – if I have to accompany you to your bedroom.'

She shrugged and went with him into his study. It was a room that she hardly ever entered nowadays, and never for more than the briefest minute, to deliver a message or borrow a book from the shelves. She thought it unlikely that she had sat down there since the day of their quarrel twelve years ago. She did not even use this telephone, for the household had a separate line upstairs. And she usually conducted transactions connected with her income through Mr. Quinn in the outer office. So now she felt the disadvantage of strangeness, although she liked the room and had always liked it. She thought that it expressed those qualities of Tom which his manner sought to conceal: his professional integrity and good sense, and his liking for order and comeliness.

She crossed to a green leather armchair by the window. Tom took off his spectacles and put them carefully into their case. He picked up a cigar.

'Do you mind if I smoke this?' She shook her head. 'Will you smoke?'

He came to her very politely with the cigarette box, but she shook her head again. She was angry with him for trapping her at an 'off' moment, and she told herself that she was far too tired to be interested in whatever play-acting was toward. She sat very still and watched him clip and light his cigar. After the first pull he turned and looked at her again.

'You ought to have some tea,' he said. 'Is there anyone in the kitchen, if I rang?'

'There certainly isn't.'

'Could you find the things and make some yourself?'

'I could, but I don't want any. Say what you have to say, Tom. I'm tired. Have my dividends gone down at sea, or has Aunt Hannah cut me out of her will?'

'Neither of these things has occurred.'

'Well then – *why* are you looking so much the family lawyer?'

'I suppose because I *am* the family lawyer, damn it!'

She said no more. Obviously he was agitated and would have to be given his head. He moved about the room with exaggerated lordliness, replaced one or two books in the shelves, poured himself out some whiskey.

'No use offering you this?'

'No.'

'Brandy?'

'No, thank you.'

He crossed to her suddenly, took her hand and felt the wet handkerchief which was clutched in it. He dropped it at once and walked away, smiling at her surprised annoyance.

'More tears than are usually shed in "mere femininity",' he said. 'Did I startle witness? I wish I'd been a barrister, Nell. I'd have loved to lead for the Crown in a *cause célèbre.* Defence is too romantic. Prosecution is the thing, and F.E.

Smith was the boyo to conduct it! I'd have been as good, I think, after my own manner –'

'If you've dragged me in here to listen to your might-have-been daydreams, Tom –'

'Sorry, Nell. Your tears are none of my business, I suppose?'

'No.'

'All right. I accept that. But the fact is that I'm not inhuman, and if they should by any chance bear any relation to the – the matter I wish to discuss – well, that may be awkward.'

Nell thought that he was beginning to enjoy himself, and clearly at her expense. Occasionally through the years one or other of them staged such trivial and punctilious bickers as this, she saw, was going to be. The idea was mildly to wound, decorously to deflate. The impulse would rise unexpectedly from some trifle, but its source in both was an unsleeping need for vengeance. She knew that, and recognised in Tom a consanguineous strain of resemblance to her, in this as in other things, that made her glad enough they had not married. Tonight evidently he wanted to annoy her. It was a pity that she was too tired to do battle, and give him his fun.

It was obvious that the instigation of whatever was coming was her friendship with Matt Costello. This was odd. He had never before appeared to notice the existence of her male admirers. The occasional bouts of fencing by which they coldly and tacitly reminded each other that the old injury was not forgotten never arose from anything which possibly be interpreted as jealousy in Tom. They might cross swords about her job as History mistress which he disapproved of, or about her activities in relation to religious charities in the town, or about books or politics or his coarse vocabulary; sometimes they could quarrel coolly over simple domestic matters, such as the dismissal or not of a cook, or whether he really required as much whiskey as he consumed. They found occasions of asperity with ease as they required them – but 'Nell's followers' as Una called them, were not among these.

However, about Matt Tom had taken an erratic line which sometimes amused and stimulated Nell in irrational moments but which on reflection she could not explain. He was not jealous. How could he be? In the nine years since her return from Italy he and she had lived under one roof, and if he had the faintest impulse of possessiveness about her within that time he would have shown it. He had not done so. If he had ever really wanted her – she was here, and he could have tried his luck. He had not done so. Therefore to suspect him now of any kind of jealousy was idiotic. Such dog-in-the-manger nonsense would be insane, hysterical – and Tom was neither of those things. Yet sometimes she saw that his eye, moving from her to Matt, was cold with an unusual coldness, and he took rather elaborate care to represent his old friend, both in his hearing and behind his back, as a notorious and unrepentant Don Juan. And all through June it had seemed to Nell that he disapproved of her visits to Weir House, and yet was vaguely suspicious of her motives when she did not go there. But Tom was the most articulate and self-willed of men, and it was impossible to doubt that if at any time he felt that he had a particular claim in anything, he would know how and when to stake it.

Nevertheless, about Matt. He had been pleased to hear of his return. He remembered him affectionately from youth, and had always been generous in praise of him, and inclined to tell generous tales of Costello's young exploits and talents. Matt's career interested him; he bought and defended all his books, which he admired – with detachment, but sincerely. He had argued Nell into a rage more than once when she attacked them. So he had looked forward to meeting him again, and clearly at first contact he and Matt felt the authenticity of their old liking and appreciated each other. But that, it seemed, was as far as they could get. They developed no real desire for each other's society and their friendship, frequently promising for a minute or two, never actually warmed. Something impalpable stood between them, and made them feline when together, Matt as well as Tom. Nell was always aware of their claws now when they conversed. There was something secretly exciting to her in this consciousness, but she knew her rather contemptible pleasure to be irrational. A false fire lighted by conceit. Heavens, with what mockery Tom would view such a schoolgirl misreading of his attitude to Matt! Yet what *was* his grudge against the man? And what on earth was he going to say now?

'You've described me as the family lawyer. Well I am in a sense your guardian, Nell.'

'My guardian?' She laughed. 'I was thirty-three in April.'

'Oh, I know all that. What I mean is that I happen to be the head of the family, the male head –'

'Yes, Tom.'

She said this so politely that he glared at her for a second before proceeding.

'– and in that capacity I propose to lecture you.'

'I deny the right of the head of any family to lecture me.'

'Don't be so silly!'

'It's you who're being silly. But if I'm ever to get to bed – what is your lecture?'

'You're getting yourself talked about in the town in connection with this Costello fellow!'

'Well –?'

'Well what?'

'Well, what are they saying?'

'How the hell do I know what they're saying? But can't you guess? You know – you're the very one who knows – what's thought of the gentleman's books in Mellick, and what his private reputation is worth here, for that matter! Indeed, I think he can count himself lucky that his return wasn't celebrated by a public demonstration and the public burning of all available copies of his works in front of the Father Mathew Memorial!'

'It now seems we're all lucky that such a demonstration was not organised by the male head of the Mahoneys!'

'Be serious, girl. It's you I'm thinking of. And before I go on to what really matters, here's something that doesn't bother me much, but may bother you. You, Nell, one of this town's shining lights, star turn of the Vincent de Paul and head cook and bottle-washer of the Legion of Mary, you're setting a fine example lately to the flappers and corner girls of Mellick! Oh yes, I know they have a halo on you already, and that Ceesar's wife was the town trollop to you –'

'Really Tom –'

'– but still, gadding into movies and up the mountainsides with an immoral, loose-living writer whose works we are all prohibited to read! How is that going to appear to the chaste eyes of the Knights of Saint Joseph, will you tell me?'

'You tell me. They've evidently been running round to discuss it all with you.'

'They have not.'

'Then where do you get your news?'

'I have no specific news. My mother's dear old friends are no buddies of mine. But a straw can tell you where the wind sits, and by the hints that Father Malachi is dropping – as loud as bombs, God help him! –'

'Father Malachi dropping hints about me! – He ought to be ashamed of himself!'

'Father Malachi has nothing in this world to be ashamed of.'

'If he's turning into a town gossip, he has that to be ashamed of.'

Tom took a slow and careful drink of whiskey. He was muddling this situation and he knew it. With fury he knew it. For weeks he had been fighting with an insane desire to quarrel with Nell, and punch the head off Matt Costello. He hardly admitted the craving to his intellectual self, but it fretted his blood night and day nevertheless, a hot, uneasy virulence. And last night the Franciscan's peculiar behaviour, his obvious and rather surprised liking for Matt coupled with his loyal determination to warn his friend Tom that something which he ought to value more than he appeared to was about to slip through his fingers, his innocent, embarrassed effort to convey this warning while being fair to both hearers – all this made it clear that the town was interested in Nell and Matt. Father Malachi was a saintly creature who spoke no evil of anyone, and rarely heard it – for the reason that most of the salacious-minded knew better than to risk the trouncings he would be delighted to give them. If he dropped hints, then they certainly did not arise from silly murmurings about Matt's evil character or Nell's possible inclination to loose living – but simply meant that Mellick was match-making with amiable innocence, and probably thinking that the famous Mr. Costello would be a very suitable *parti* for the intellectual Miss Mahoney and wouldn't it be lucky for him now if he married a good, Catholic girl like that who'd teach him sense and stop him writing those unpleasant bits in his books? Which was probably what Malachi was thinking, but with regret for his friend Tom, who ought not to be allowed unwarned to lose a pearl he had never valued.

Tom knew all that, and in the midst of his rage had been touched and amused by the awkward efforts of the big, ascetic Franciscan to play the coquettish tea-cup game. Now therefore to drag the innocent creature up as villain of a non-existent slander-drama was, the lawyer knew, a senseless failure in technique. But tonight he was beyond all patience. During the evening, waiting in this room for the sound of her car outside, her step in the hall; knowing her at Weir House where Costello was, and finding every five minutes an hour, driven at last to the indignity of going out to watch for her approach up King Street – then seeing her come up the steps to him, in tears! By God, the thing was out of hand at last and he past all finesse! But when he ordered her into the study, having 'things to say,' he knew very well, and came near laughing at himself for it, that he had no idea what on earth to say, but simply had to kick up a row. Certainly the rubbish he had spouted in the last five minutes did him no credit, and got no one anywhere. And now he had dragged poor Malachi in as the –in-the-woodpile! God! Was he taking leave of his senses? He might be twenty-one, so irrational was his every word tonight!

And there she sat, where she had sat the night that he had asked her to be his wife. It was winter then, the curtains were drawn behind her and the glow of the fire had warmed the lamplight falling on her face. But it was the same chair. There she sat, disturbing the room with her strange, living grace.

'Let Malachi alone. He's done you no harm. But if he's being old-maidishly coy – God bless his innocence – about Mr. Costello's "attentions" to you, what do you think the poison-ivies of this town are saying?'

'I really can't imagine – or care. What are you getting at, Tom?'

'Here's what. Don't get yourself involved with Costello without knowing what you're doing, that's all. You know his work – and I'll say this for it, I think it's perfectly sincere. I think it contains his philosophy – his moral philosophy, which is not yours. Apart from that, he has lived as he chose – good luck to him! But he's a notorious womaniser. It's not for nothing that he analyses emotion and sensuality with such skill! He is a womaniser and a pagan, and he's at present deep in some illicit affair in London about which – when you are out of earshot, naturally! – he is singularly ponderous and sentimental. Moreover, as a type he is neither a marrying man, Nell, nor the sort of patient, good-natured old-time Irish 'flirt' that you may be accustomed to!'

She leant forward and took a cigarette.

'I have been warned,' she said.

'Of course, he has you flattered silly. Oh, he's sophisticated, experienced, famous. He's even fairly brainy. He has nothing to do over here and you're very easy on the eye. And he has a knack. He's a romantic! In a world of realities and nightmares, in a doomed, preoccupied and desperate world, he has the smug cunning to stand aside and be a romantic, so help me! The last of the romantics!'

'Yes. He has a knack. There's this to be said for the romantic attitude, Tom, that at least it is romantic.'

'Then – you actually like him?'

'I like him immensely.'

There was silence. Tom paced up and down the room. He would have said that he was afraid of no one on earth, but he had always been timid before this quiet adversary. And now he was terrified, not so much of her as of what she had just said. He found himself unable to think; he plunged for any retort.

'You like him? A bastard who can do nothing better than make you cry?'

'*He* didn't make me cry.'

'Oh no! I suppose Will and Una made nasty faces at you! When were you last so abandoned as to shed tears in the street, may I ask?'

'I sometimes did when I was living in Rome,' she said.

The unexpected answer steadied him, though he had not the courage to examine yet what it might mean. Simply it rang a memory. It was the first hint that she had ever dropped that she, too, remembered something of their past. He took a little courage.

'Nell,' he said gently, 'what is the situation between you and Costello?'

'What on earth does it matter to you, Tom? And by what right do you try to force my confidence?'

He became angry again.

'By no bloody right whatever – but through the sheer force of natural indignation, let me tell you!'

'Indignation? I can't see –'

'Oh no, you can't see! You're as blind as a lovely little kitten, poor, dear Nell! But a man who was once turned down hard by you for one decently conducted moral lapse may be allowed to marvel at your present complaisance towards a thorough-paced, self-confessed seducer!'

So he *is* a hysterical dog-in-the-manger, Nell was thinking. He doesn't want me, but no one else is to have me, so help him God! Her mouth curled angrily, and she decided to let him have whatever punishment she could. She wished she had much more to hurl. She wished she had vengeance in her pocket now.

'He hasn't seduced *me,*' she said.

Tom stared at her as if he feared she was going out of her mind.

'My God!' he said. 'My God! Will you *try* to talk like yourself, Nell?'

'I had thought he might want to – though your term is a little absurd at my age.'

'You *had* thought he might want to! Great Christ! You *had* thought he might want to – and so you put in as much time as you could strolling and driving about with him!'

'I told you at the beginning of all this commotion that I'm thirty-three.'

'And on my soul you'd need to tell me! Thirty-three – and you're talking – you're talking like a tough little débutante in one of those way-back Lonsdale plays!'

'I don't remember Lonsdale's plays,' she said politely.

'In the name of Almighty God, will you pull yourself together and be Nell Mahoney for just five seconds?'

'I don't want to be anyone. I want to go to bed. I don't know what all this is about, Tom. You began it, and I wish you'd finish it.'

There was a pause. Tom cleared his throat, took up his whiskey glass and put it down again without drinking.

'I'm trying to guard you against your own feelings, Nell. I hadn't thought you had any feelings worth bothering about. You made it clear to me once that you were very shallow indeed. But now – now it seems that you have emotions of some sort, or anyhow a peculiar kind of vanity which may actually tempt you to make a fool of yourself pretty much as people of feeling do. Surprising, but there it is. I'm not as vengeful a man as I'd like to be, Nell, and much as you deserve to be well and truly hurt, for once in your stand-off life, I'd rather not see it happen. I'd rather not see you give your feelings, such as they are, into the charge of a wanderer, a ladykiller, a pleasure-seeker like Costello.'

'I think you're the most hypocritical windbag I've ever listened to, Tom.'

He shrugged.

'Of course, if you're going to sink to sheer abuse!'

He moved uncertainly about the room. 'It's very odd. You do one man a rank injustice for something in his past which if it was in another's I take it you would have to accept as a "romantic" peccadillo. "Mere femininity", I suppose.'

'I suppose so.' She stood up. 'May I go to bed now, Tom?'

He stood directly in her path, seeming, to her, suddenly very tall and overbearing.

'Not yet,' he said. 'Eleven years ago, standing in this room you called me cad and hypocrite and lowdown heartless cheat. Ok. Since that time your sanctity, your cold-blooded, spinsterish morality and your general, all-round untouchableness have been accepted by your intimidated and edified entourage, until, hey presto! a real profligate comes along, a gentleman from the great world who has long lost count of his conquests among the virgins, peeresses and courtesans of all the capitals. The sort of finished article we can't attempt to emulate in Mellick, naturally. And we find that that is what you "like immensely", that we had somehow grossly misunderstood you! It turns out now that the shortest cut to your heart would have been through the brothels and bedrooms of Europe!'

'You're talking insanely.'

'I'm suffering from shock. Are you not going to explain your goings-on to me?'

'Matt has asked me to marry him.'

The news had a curious effect on Tom. He had been standing tense, drawn up to his full, great height, his shoulders rigid and his hands thrust deep into his coat-pockets. Now, having heard what she said, he slackened slowly, growing smaller; his hands came out of his pockets and dropped to his sides.

'To marry him?'

She nodded.

'Oh well! Oh well, in that case, you must forgive my remarks. I didn't think he was a marrying man, I thought perhaps you'd get fond of him and –'

He moved past and went and leant on the mantelpiece, fondling his whiskey glass.

'What you're saying isn't true, Tom. You didn't think that. Why shouldn't he be a marrying man?'

'Why indeed?' He spoke without turning towards her. There was silence for a second or two, and then he burst out in a savage, raging voice, still standing with his back to her.

'So he has elected to marry you! He would! I needn't have put it past him! The bumptious little literary gent! The Mellick genius! Great Christ Almighty! Three weeks, four weeks! And a mistress in London that he's ready to groan about behind your back! God knows how many lovely mistresses sighing in Paris, Vienna and Berlin! But he wants to marry *you*, no less! Of all the nerve! Of all the bloody nerve!'

'I can only think that you've had too much whiskey.'

'I have *not* had too much whiskey!' He wheeled around and she was shocked by the look of misery in his face. 'I tell you that the man has a nerve, an admirable bloody nerve, and I know what I'm talking about in this matter! I haven't watched you like a lynx these nine years for nothing! I know your pokerface – for all the good it does me! But he! By what divine perception does he read you – and work miracles? Oh God! I suppose love knows itself. But in nine long years since you came back you have never once betrayed to me, by as much as the bat of an eyelid, that you even dimly remember you once loved me. Not by a flicker or a word. And yet you did love me. You know you did. Don't dare to stand there and deny it!'

'Tom, I could never deny it. I loved you with all my heart.'

Their eyes met in helpless questioning.

'You look tired,' Tom said. And then: 'It took very little to kill your love, Nell.'

'I was very young and stupid – much more juvenile than my actual age. But you were hideously cruel to my idiotic prudery, and you know that anyway II was the deceit I minded –'

'So you remember?'

'I remember.'

'You thought I should have married that harmless little shop girl, and made a shambles of life for her and me?'

'Need we go into it now?'

'No. But taking a wife is no joke. I never wanted one at all until I wanted you, and after you fell through I never wanted any other wife.'

'Which proves that you never really wanted a wife, and that everything has turned out for the best.'

'Maybe. When are you going to marry Costello?'

'I have refused to marry him.'

'Refused?' The voice leapt. 'But you've just said you "like him immensely"?'

'Yes. And I do. But that's not the same as love – not quite the same. Still –' she turned aside from Tom's now piercing eyes and fidgeted with pencils on his desk. 'Still, I'd have chanced that. I like him quite well enough to take the chance. But – he doesn't love me enough –'

'Doesn't love you enough, Nell?'

'There's that woman in London. It's over, but she's done something to him, frightened him. He wants to stay here with me, and forget all that, and have children. I couldn't face it – I'm too jealous – I –'

'He asked you, in fact, to be his poultice, his bromide, his ever-ready medicine chest! By the Lord God!'

She laughed a little.

'It isn't quite like that. Oh, it's complicated. He's nice, Tom. And he's good – and very unhappy.'

'I'm delighted to hear that last! I'd like to have the choking of him this minute!' Tom was in shamelessly high spirits now. 'But what were you crying for when you came in? Why did he make you cry?'

'He didn't make me. I think I was crying over the wastefulness of feeling, the maddening vagueness of desires!'

'You have some sort of a yen for that fellow!'

'I like him. I've told you that.'

'Vagueness of desires,' said Tom. 'I congratulate you. I have never been vague about the sole desire of my personal life. For better or worse I have never been able to displace the absolute love I once gave to you and which you flung back in my face. I have tried to, but it was honestly impossible. So I shall die a bachelor, leaving no Mahoneys behind me to do filial reverence, because of you, fair cousin.'

She stared at him.

'That can't be true!' she said. 'It simply can't. You're inventing it now so as to get out of your dog in-the-manger scene with some kind of flourish!'

'Dog-in-the-manger?'

'Yes. You never wanted me – oh, that was obvious – until he did! Why, Tom, how could you have concealed it? I was here. You had only to speak. Oh no, I simply don't believe you! No one in their senses, no one with a vestige of love could be so cold and conceited!'

'That's what I thought about you – and *I* was right. I waited for a sign and I never got the tip of the tail of one. So I saw you were really through with me – and I was damned if I was going to come whining after you for favours you had categorically withdrawn. Besides, I'd have you know that I'm none of your modern novelists, biliously certain that it is impossible to do without what can't be had. I'm a civilised man. I can get on reasonably without the unattainable.'

'Ah, Tom! The conceit, the coldness. You're a real Irishman.'

'Are we conceited? Anyhow, it's our womenfolk who're cold. Ask any divorce lawyer or gynaecologist.'

She leant against the table desk and stared down at her toes.

'What sort of sign were you looking for? Did you expect me to propose to you?'

'No. But a little goodwill, a little inclination to my point of view, perhaps. Anyhow, less severity would have been encouraging, and less sarcasm and religiosity.'

'You created all those things in me. You frightened me silly. I was determined never to be hurt again as you hurt me. I became practically a flint in self defence.'

'Much good it did you. A smart alec from literal London has only to step your way to have you crying.'

'Oh no. It's not the same thing at all. Nothing will ever be as bad as that first year in Rome. Thank Heaven!'

'Well, evidently you buried it all very nicely in the end. And now I've said my say, and I haven't been believed. So there we are.'

She looked up at him and her eyes were wide and dark.

'If you'd only said it sooner, Tom! Any time sooner –'

'You mean before this bastard came around?'

She nodded.

He strode to her side.

'Are you meaning to tell me that if I had told you how much I love you exactly one month ago, you'd have been glad to hear it?'

'I'm glad to hear it now.'

'Oh, Nell!'

'But – he has muddled me, Tom. It's a pity. It's confusing.'

He took her hand and his voice fell to deep gentleness.

'No, it isn't confusing,' he said. 'You're not in love with him and once you did love me. I have loved you ever since I was a man and fit to. I love you now, and I will love you on my deathbed. I'm not wanting consolation from you, or oblivion or opiates of any kind – I'm asking you for the one unmitigated desire of my life. You are the one glory I have always coveted; you are all that I mean by beauty. I'm prepared to match the plain truth of that against all comers, Nell, and I beg you, I beg you to marry me.'

Nell heard his voice of eleven years ago, and his words, and smiled now a little at the echoes. He was the same. Rich and formal in feeling, very traditional, every inch a man. She looked up wonderingly into his lighted face.

THE TENTH CHAPTER

Dinner would be late. The children had insisted on going into Mellick with Una in the afternoon, to buy goodbye presents for Uncle Matt. And on their return the excitement of presentation in the drawing room had been prolonged. Una had let them have their heads over the business, as it eased their sweet and real disappointment about their uncle's sudden departure. The fuss and chatter was a help to Matt too, she thought, as well as to her and Will, who were feeling perplexed and saddish.

It seemed that Matt had had a letter from his theatrical agent that morning which made it clear that he must sail for New York at once to discuss production arrangements there for one of his plays. If he got to London by Wednesday morning he could probably catch the *Normandie* on Saturday. Pleased by the children's grief at his going and in no mood for his own exclusive company he had planned a method of departure which enchanted them. The garage from which he had hired his car would provide a driver to take him to Dublin the next morning, and with him Una and, as it had been settled after much disputing, Liam, Maire and Sean. There was to be a magnificent day in Dublin – lunch at Jammet's, shopping, a movie. At the end of it they would all drive to Dún Laoghaire to see Matt on to the mail boat and, as he sailed out of Dublin Bay his sad but, he imagined, exhausted relations would turn their faces south for home. Una shook her head over the plan, but saw that he was determined upon it, and was too sorry for him to argue much.

Neither she nor Will believed in the agent's letter. There had been a letter, yes; but not announcing that he must leave for London and New York at once. Matt had waved an envelope at them, but he had not unfolded its contents in their presence or tossed it over to them to read. It was true that he had expected to have to go to America in the autumn, and Una was not sufficiently informed in theatrical custom to think the last days of June an odd time for Broadway to become impatient to prepare a new production. But – after Matt had in her hearing last night asked Nell to come down to the weir, Una had not seen him again until he came to her in the garden this morning, with his morning mail in his hands and his neat, regretful story of imminent flight upon his lips. Una was sorry. Nell had not come into the house last night to say good night, and Will, hearing her car depart, had raised his brows at his wife. Going to bed the two had talked carefully of Knockabree Belle and the July cattle sales and Sean's inclination to stammer. Una knew well the joy it would be to Will to have Matt stay at home and marry her sister. Today she was feeling somewhat annoyed with Nell. Was Will's famous brother not good enough for her ladyship? It was puzzling. Even yesterday Una had not thought that Matt and Nell were so near a crisis in their friendship. She wondered what was said in that long debate by the weir last night, and knew that she would never be told. Anyhow, Nell was clearly impossible about men.

The drawing room was littered with tissue paper and 'novelties.' Liam's gift, which ravished the donor, was a very tricky cigarette box. If you pressed one lever of this gay box a dainty little feminine hand shot out and presented you with a cigarette. If you pressed the other lever a much smaller little feminine hand popped out with a match. A real 'novelty,' in examination of which Will had perpetrated a mild *gaffe*: 'My dear chap, it's marvellous,' he said to Matt, 'it does away with all necessity for a wife.' But Liam's meditative comment had been helpful. 'Yes, Daddy,' he said, 'it really does, up to a point.' Maire, unlucky to the end, had chosen a tie in doubtful taste; Sean and Peadar had clubbed together to give the writer a box of variegated pencils, and Una Bán's present, selected by Liam, who had inside information about the recipient's likes, was two handkerchiefs from Woolworths bearing portraits of Lord Baldwin and President Roosevelt.

'Will your flat be in order and ready for you, Matt?' Una asked.

'Oh, I'm not going to South Square. My man's on holiday – and anyway I intend to give it up. I'll go to a hotel for these days.'

'Give it up?'

'Yes – Gray's Inn is a bit off the map, and if you're all going to come and stay with me – you've sworn you will, haven't you, Liam? – I'II want a bigger place.'

'Oh – I liked that flat.'

'So did I, Una, but I'm tired of it now. I'll put my things in store, and when I get back from America I'll be a millionaire and I'll take an apartment in Brook House.'

'Well, then, we'll certainly come to stay. Really, children, if we're ever to dine, you *must* go to bed. Give Matt some sherry, Will. Yes, Liam, to bed. We have to be up at dawn tomorrow for this Dublin expedition.'

'Oh yes! Little did I know this time yesterday that I'd actually be in Dublin tomorrow!'

'It's my first time,' said Maire.

'And mine,' said Sean.

'Was I ever in Dublin, Daddy?' asked Peadar.

'I've been in Jammet's twice before,' said Liam. 'Haven't I, Mother?'

'It's very vulgar to boast,' said Una.

'Lucky it's holidays,' he went on. 'I suppose you'd never have let us go, darling, if we were still doing exams?'

'Certainly not! Fancy upsetting your exams!'

'The big girls are still doing them at St. Anne's,' said Maire. 'Aunt Nell has to be at school until Wednesday, I think.'

Will had had to open and decant a bottle of sherry.

'Here you are, Matt. We really ought to have had a bit of a party tonight.'

'I did telephone to Nell at lunchtime,' Una said, 'and suggested her dining here, but she is having to attend some wretched end-of-term concert at St. Anne's, she said. She sent you *bon voyage* and all that, Matt. She was sorry and surprised, as we all are.'

Will admired the smooth, face-saving tact of this speech. He knew that Una had not suggested to Nell anything so embarrassing as that she should dine with them that night. Also he guessed that his wife believed Nell less surprised by her news of Matt than perhaps she had hoped she sounded.

'Will you say goodbye to her for me, Una?'

'It's a pity you won't see Aunt Nell kill her first salmon with that lovely rod, Uncle Matt. Can I have some sherry, Daddy?'

'No, Liam; no, sir.'

'Ah, thank God, here's Bridie. Off with the lot of you now. Yes, Uncle Matt will come up with me after dinner. Won't you, Matt?'

'Yes. And I must put all my presents in a safe place. Good night, *au revoir* – good night.'

Matt sipped his sherry and looked down towards the weir and the shining river, more hidden now by the density of green than when he had arrived. He was thinking of Tom's ironic quoting of *Ulysses* ... 'He returns after a life of absence to that spot of earth where he was born ...' After a life of absence – there's the rub. A life of absence predicates a life of absence. And as for the mulberry tree and all that mockery, there was no sense in planting anymore. Life was grown rotten with its own fruits and even if I happened to be Shakespeare, I couldn't save the world. It is beyond all saviours, and the Bard was never one. Going back. Going back alone into the places of doom and panic and despair. Going back into a life where there were no values to fit the heart – save one, completely irrelevant and forever withdrawn. Going back to seek an objective he could never accept, to make money he did not need in a world full of needs beyond human management. What was there to do when all escapes were barred and mankind's panorama ahead was what it was? Merely write, and in due course die. Oh, green and trim Free State! Smug, obstinate and pertinacious little island, your sins and ignorances are thick upon your face, and thickening under the authority of your 'sea-green incorruptible!' But your guilts seem positively innocent, your ignorances are perhaps wisdom when measured against the general European plight. How odd if the distressful country, the isle of Saints and Doctors from which Patrick banished snakes, should prove a last oasis, a floating Lotus Land when the floods rise! The harmony within this house, for instance – is that representative and does it promise anything? This uncrowded landscape, flowing peace. This easy sense of God and of right and wrong, with the fastidiousness and curious courage that such possessions give. God save Ireland. There might conceivably be some general hope in such a salvage.

'You ought to have seen Tom today,' said Will. 'He'll be disgusted with you, tearing off like this.'

'I'm sorry not to have seen him, but –'

Tom. What a fool of a man, with all his irony and self-sufficiency. A fool indeed in that last – never a greater.

Will refilled their glasses and lifting his own smiled with great affection at his brother.

'Come back to us soon,' he said, 'and here's long life to *The Heart of Stone.*'

The curtain must be up now, Matt thought; it was after half-past eight. She was standing in the wings, waiting to make that first great, summery entrance. He would see her do that once more, would see his whole play. He would sit alone at the back of the stalls while she believed seas swung between them safely still. But she need not trouble. There would be no sign and the seas would flow forever. Yet for once he would sit and watch her as a stranger might – a thing he had never done. And then – the *Normandie.*

They went in to dinner. The evening was grey and chilly now; Una raised the flames of lamps and lighted candles. Roses swooned in beauty on the table; the brood mares and the silver trophies kept their ancient places; beyond the window lay childhood's unchanged garden.

Will was hungry and Una was glad to have him so. 'He's a very difficult man to feed,' she told Matt, 'though he thinks he's so easy.'

Will smiled at her and Matt felt a spasm of boredom, almost of outrage. This rounded-off contentment, this imperturbable and well-earned peace! Oh Heaven! Nell had not this suavity. He looked at her empty chair and thought of her grave, strange face. Nell knew the touch of the sword and was a little mad.

'What are you smiling at, Matt?'

'I was thinking of *Don Quixote,* Una. Have you ever read it?'

'No, and please don't give it to me. Tom did once. It's an absolutely deadly book – I don't care what you say.'

Bridgham-Groombridge,
July-December, 1937.

THE END

KATE O'BRIEN

Kate O'Brien, 1936
Arlen House Archive

Kate O'Brien's books:

Distinguished Villa (1926), play
Without My Cloak (1931), novel
The Ante-Room (1934), novel
Mary Lavelle (1936), novel
Farewell Spain (1937), political travelogue
Pray for the Wanderer (1938), novel
The Land of Spices (1941), novel
The Last of Summer (1943), novel
English Diaries and Journals (1943), literary criticism
That Lady (1946), novel
That Lady: A Romantic Drama (1949), play
Teresa of Avila (1951), biography
The Flower of May (1953), novel
As Music and Splendour (1958), novel
My Ireland (1962), travelogue
Presentation Parlour (1963), biography